THE ORANGE NOTEBOOKS

Praise for The Orange Notebooks

"*The Orange Notebooks* is stunning and luminous, a story that cuts back and forth in time to uncover the mysteries of Anna's passion and grief. In lovely and intrepid writing, Susanna Crossman has given us a fiercely observed novel of shimmering beauty and loss, a deeply affecting meditation on ways that love can transcend unspeakable sadness."

—Luanne Rice, author of *The Shadow Box* and *Last Day*

"Susanna Crossman brings a poet's sensibility and great wisdom to her examination of a mother's grief on the loss of her young son. Lyrical, moving, and masterful, this book, at its heart, is about love—for those who know us well, for those we hold most dear—and how we manage when that love is lost."

—Rachel Cantor, author of *Half-Life of a Stolen Sister*

Praise for Susanna Crossman's previous work

"Vivid and poignant... A powerful memoir of a particularly unusual childhood... Concrete, disturbing and moving."—*The Observer*

"Vivid and painfully honest ... Painful to read but so beautifully done ... There's something of the Levy sensibility here. It's serious and poetic. It's delicate and wise. It's a multilayered excavation, a rich but also careful unfolding of the truth."—*Sunday Times*

"In the changing waters of memory... Susanna Crossman navigates between cosy mystery and Gothic novel, in a spooky debut book on the class struggle."—*Monde des Livres (Le Monde)*

"Served by a precise and sharp language, this first novel delivers a fairly revealing portrait of English society, between disillusions, excesses and withdrawal into oneself. An author to follow, without a doubt."

—*Alibi Magazine*

THE ORANGE NOTEBOOKS

SUSANNA CROSSMAN

PRINCE EDWARD COUNTY, ONTARIO

First published in 2025 by Bluemoose Books Ltd.

Library and Archives Canada Cataloguing in Publication
Title: The orange notebooks / Susanna Crossman.
Names: Crossman, Susanna, author.
Identifiers: Canadiana (print) 20250211777 | Canadiana (ebook) 20250215136 | ISBN 9781998336197 (softcover) | ISBN 9781998336203 (EPUB)
Subjects: LCGFT: Diary fiction. | LCGFT: Novels.
Classification: LCC PR6103.R53 O73 2025 | DDC 823/.92—dc23

Published by Assembly Press | assemblypress.ca
Cover and interior designed by Greg Tabor

Printed and bound in Canada on uncoated paper made from 100% recycled content in line with our commitment to ethical business practices and sustainability.

"Life always says Yes and No simultaneously."
Rainer Maria Rilke, *The Dark Interval*

"A touch of madness is, I think, almost always necessary for constructing a destiny."
Marguerite Yourcenar, *With Open Eyes: Conversations With Matthieu Galey*

Contents

Draft Archive Note:
The Orange Notebooks

I received the enclosed from former patient No. 123A78 at the Hôpital Psychiatrique du Val, France. These English-language papers, referred to as *The Orange Notebooks,* arrived in July 2014, a year after she'd left. She requested anonymity—she calls herself Anna. The patient was diagnosed with clinical depression and PTSD (see DSM-5 and my notes): depression, hyperarousal, delusion, and moderate paranoia. (These papers contain much more than the above—life is stranger than anything a doctor's mind could invent!)

The patient's breakdown was triggered by the death of her son, Louis. In her accompanying letter, Anna writes, "Lou's death was time—there was a before and an after..." The notebooks document her four months at the hospital, but also her relationship with Louis's father, a record of a bright life between London and France, crossing the Channel, "a liquid bridge," and the journey she took in June 2013 with another patient. The latter was part of Anna's delusional conviction that she would meet her son again. She entered what she called "an upside-down world," and went to rescue Louis, thinking she could put the world back the right way up.

During our appointments, it often seemed this patient sought a different language, engaging in the natural world and colours to find answers to her tragedy. I regularly wondered about her dance with death, for grief is not a mental illness. In our society, death has become taboo, and a child's death often carries a great silencing. We must question whether, if we knew how to die, how to cope with death, we would be better at living. After over forty years of hospital work, when confronted by human pain, I still feel like an explorer shining a torch into a cave, hoping to find a precious stone, a remedy. These notebooks are an illuminating account of a curative journey, Anna's map to get "to the other side. Because I refuse—absolutely—to let go of life."

Dr. Vidonne, Hôpital Psychiatrique du Val, France, July 2014

1. We've Only Just Begun

I remember this:

We've just got off the Channel ferry. On the motorway, we're heading to London. In the backseat, you say:

"Mama! Mama! The wire things are round and then go straight."

"Sorry, I can't hear." I overtake a yellow Spanish lorry, glare at the driver beeping his horn. "Speak up, *buba*," I yell, tired from the overnight crossing. I didn't sleep.

"Mama, the wire things!" you shout. "The wire things are round and then go straight!"

"Be quiet, *buba*. I am driving!"

A sports car with the number-plate LUV U is close behind me. The driver flashes his lights.

"But Mama, the wire things by the road..."

In the rear mirror, I see your small finger. From your car seat, it points to a pylon. By the road, the wires reach into the horizon. Heading out to nowhere, they seem to come from the sea. The past is behind us, I think, and wish I was still on the night boat, being cradled by the swell. Briny billows. Sailing into great waters— You interrupt my daydreams:

"Mama, the wires go round and then straight."

Glancing up, I notice that from a distance, the curves dangle like crescent moons. As we approach, the wires seem to flatten into straight lines. In my mirror, the lines continue and then disappear.

"That's an optical illusion." I explain, because I am a mother and, *buba,* it is my job to give you instructions about the workings of life. I try to tell you the rules, about danger and love, and all the things we cannot see. "An optical illusion means things are different to how they appear. An optical illusion."

"An illusion. An illusion," you repeat.

I look up at a road sign. We're sixty-three miles from London, yet already I can smell Edgware pollution and fried fish, and I feel the dry powder on my mum's skin.

In the back of the car, you whisper, over and over again:

"Illusion... illusion... illusion."

"Illusion" is an eighties song by the group Imagination. One of my mum's favourite tunes. As I drive on the motorway, it echoes in my ears. The world is just an illusion.

It is June. Two years later. France. Early afternoon. I go to ring the bell. A bee flies past my ear, landing on the brass door handle. Six black legs. A quiver of fur. In my mind, thoughts swarm of nectar, of the honey cake my Aunty Deb baked, a bittersweet mouthful, swallowed and gone. For an instant, I wonder about bee-killing pesticides, bee stings, pain, and draw back my hand. In Europe, there are almost two thousand species of bees. I know they are under threat. Recoiling, I think of the movie Lou watched, hour after hour, as children do in the comfort of evermore. The film, *Bee Movie,* portrayed bees as humans: the bee mummies and bee daddies with two bee children. Bee mornings. Bee afternoons. Clean bee nights. Bee school. Bee work. Bee retirement. Bee conformity. Bee longings. Bee love and bee hate. This humanising of the natural world is an outrageous anthropomorphic act we must not forget. The bee world has its own mystery: bees are born. Bees die. The bees are dead. The bees are buzzing. The thoughts rattle inside me. I am an empty can. No filling. No stuffing. A mother with a dead child is no longer. A mother with a dead child is a joke.

Closing my eyes, I listen to the bees. They are flying through labyrinths of grey-green stalks, gathering pollen from pale mauve blooms. The scent of lavender coats the air. A slick veneer. The sudden heat of French summers. Siesta hour. Sweat trickles down my back; the drops draw damp lines. There is an orchestral stillness, a muffled silence I know well. It seems like an odd moment to come back, while the whole world is sleeping. As though everyone is waiting, and here I am. Finally, *de retour* with the lavender, the sunflowers and the fig tree in the garden. Even the cicadas seem to be resting; the only thing I hear is bees. Some legends say bees never sleep and they go on and on making honey.

Over ten years ago, on the only occasion that we met, my late Basque mother-in-law, Katixa, gave me fair warning about bees. Inside the kitchen of her cold two-hundred-year-old house, nestled in the Spanish Pyrenees, we drank hot cups of moss-coloured verbena tea sweetened with chestnut honey. Outside, mist collected on every corner. It hung over the half-timbered house, drifted in green valleys, and shrouded the steep mountain peaks. Rain fell in a soft drizzle. Water coated everything, and it felt like we were floating inside a cloud. At her table, Katixa turned to me. Her grey hair was short and neat round her heavy face. Placing her hand on my shoulder, she said to me quietly in French, for it was the only language that we shared:

"Anna, when any death occurs you must go and tell the bees. You should knock gently on the hives. Inform them of the passing. Tell them the name of the deceased and their age. You must not forget to ask the bees politely to produce wax. Their wax will make the candles to light the path of the deceased, so they may travel safely to the other side."

In the garden, I am wondering whether the bees have been informed, when I am startled by Antton opening the door. On my way here, I practised a speech to tell him: 1) where I had been; 2) what had changed; 3) what I had understood. But he looks furious, and I step back and trip over my suitcase. Before I can say "*bonjour*" or "hello," Antton blurts out:

"I can't believe you've finally come home." Shaking his head, he strides back inside. Behind my sunglasses, tears form. Antton cannot see, which is a relief. These *lunettes* make my face feel at home. Inside here, I am safe. Some things shouldn't be opened. Outside there are monsters, sieges, and storms.

I step into the hallway of our house. My feet shuffle and hesitate. One of them inside and the other out. Suitcase in hand. Seven years earlier when we bought La Place, the estate agent described it as "*un petit château perdu.*" We joked about, "our little lost castle," bought cheap due to a leaky roof and bad wiring, miles away from everything, except for the farm down the hill. The farm called Devant-La-Place, In-Front-of-The-Place. It is time to come home. Where to begin?

Antton paces the stone corridor in his beige trench coat. Underneath, he wears a white-ironed shirt, dark trousers, and trainers with the laces tied in neat knots. His hair swept back. New white strands in the black. He looks older, like something I once read about becoming a whisper of a man. Yet he's still carelessly refined. After all this time, I have never understood how he remains elegant in all circumstances: working and living, birth and death. But it is the trench coat that worries me.

As he walks it flaps around him, fabric brushes against fabric and makes a swish, swish sound. The coat is too severely belted for such a hot day and should be worn unbuttoned. I want to warn him: the belt is a tightening noose. By the granite staircase he turns, pulls on the buckle. The beige colour is insipid to my eyes. I feel it gnawing in my stomach, and however much I reason with myself this feeling will not go away. Antton's mouth twitches, as it does when he is angry,

"I'm going into town for a school meeting."

"Could I come in with you?" I ask. "We could talk in the car. I can wait while you work..."

He nods and comes toward me, smelling of coffee and cologne. He kisses me. Not on the lips. His kisses land on my cheeks. Two times. Old school. *La bise.* Inside I smile, but sadly, I've always liked his formal ways. It is one of the reasons I fell in love with him, his mixture of ceremony and despair, and his ability to quote philosophy and poetry, lines of Heidegger, Foucault, Plato, and Celan. "We are made of words," Antton said, and we joked that we had grown up in bookless houses and were building our own library in the *château,* and that books belonged to everybody and books could change the world. We knew that once you were inside a single book it led to other books. Each single book was a library, a universe. Long ago, word after word fell in a delicate rain, and the words became a lake from which we drew our water.

"How are you?" I move backwards. I can't touch the beige coat; I don't want to get too near. Antton shrugs his shoulders and takes in my tracksuit trousers, crumpled T-shirt, dirty hair. The shades. The journey to get here was long. I hope he cannot smell the whisky on my breath. The bottle is in my suitcase, wrapped in clothes, stiff with salt water. But I will not drink again.

"I can't believe you've finally come home," Antton repeats, but this time with less anger and more defeat, and I want to take him in my arms and apologize. But he adds, "I'm leaving in thirty minutes. Don't be late," and disappears into the kitchen.

It is a struggle to carry my suitcase up the limestone steps. At the bottom are things waiting to be taken upstairs (a blue jumper, a stack of unpaid bills, a screwdriver, and a plug). At the top, I know there will be things ready to be taken down. For seven years stuff has ascended and descended this way.

Now, my legs wobble as I notice Antton has added more books to the piles on each stone step: a new biography of Freud, editions of the local newspaper, *Sud-Ouest.* A copy of *Orpheus* by Cocteau with lithographs. This play, I once told a class, was "Inspired by the Greek myth of a grieving troubadour, his descent to Hades—a *katabasis*—to find Eurydice, his dead wife. It's been revamped a million times. The story told a different way. Cocteau included mirrors—troubling gateways to the underworld."

"Greek and Roman gambling," Antton called the classic myths. "Gods playing at the cosmic game of life."

Snakes and ladders, I think, heading upstairs, everything rises and falls, comes and goes. But the Ancients are still everywhere. Our shelves are lined with *les belles lettres,* red volumes and mustard copies of the Orphic hymns. "Your house is like a bookshop," visitors joke. But, as I reach the landing, dust jackets curl, and piles of books topple onto the floor. All the paper feels suffocating, and in the heat, it smells of mildew as though mould has attacked the core. Antton has accumulated stuff while I was away; he's been building a shelter to hide from the storm.

At the top step, my foot hits the corner of a stacked collection of second-hand French detective novels: *Cet homme est dangereux* by Peter Cheyney and *Pas d'orchidées pour Miss Blandish* by James Hadley Chase. Covers show revolvers, cadavers, and long stockinged legs. Each *Série Noire* is printed in yellow and black. Books striped like buzzing bees. It makes sense, I think. My Basque mother-in-law was right. The bees need to be informed.

Outside our son's room, Antton has piled more dusty cardboard boxes. Inside one is a collection of Basque comic books written in the Latin alphabet that Antton always wishes he knew. Glancing over, I see the comic books are stories of separatists, berets, and gastronomy. Witches and mountain cheese. I wonder why he's bought books that no one in our house can read. Antton often tells people, "All I have from the Basque language are the two awkward T's in the spelling of my name." But I picture these T's like trees with outspread branches. They hold his centre.

Wiping the sweat from my forehead, I go into Lou's room, put my suitcase down, and slide onto his bed. Around me are Lou's toys, clothes, and his drawing stuff. Everything is the same yet Lou isn't here. He is gone. My Lou is gone. Months have passed since I last lay here, but the grief remains, and it falls on me, a tumble of pain. If I could give it a shape it would be a boulder, a weight. Every day, I topple. Every day, I'm felled. Yet, his death has been easier when I am beneath this rock, resting in the dirt, next to Lou.

"It is more suitable," I told my psychiatrist, Dr. Vidonne, in one of my first sessions, "when I don't try to pretend things are normal."

On his bed, I ache for him, in my heart, my belly, my womb. Twenty-two bones in my head miss him, and the rough grain of my senses remembers his skin. Those two square metres that my doctor friend Rachel told me are the largest bodily sense organ. Cutaneous receptors captured Lou's touch, the feel of his small fingers, and his arms tight around me, tickles and hugs. My baby is stuck in my deep skin, absorbing shock.

A crack runs across the ceiling plaster, reaching the light. The dangling lampshade is patterned with stars, and it sets me thinking of orientation, and the damp map in my suitcase. Yann gave it to me on our very last morning together, to show me our path and *notre destin.*

"There must be hope," Yann insisted, and traced our journey on the blue paper sea. At the port, we prepared to leave as the sun rose. Beneath the dawn sky everything was still, and we could never have imagined what would happen that day. On the deck, Yann's eyes scanned the waves. "Don't forget. Without hope we cannot breathe."

Clutching the duvet, hope shifts inside me. Things have changed, and I don't want them to be the same.

During the weeks I was away, I often pictured Lou's room. Late at night, or early morning, when I couldn't sleep, I imagined my head on his pillow, the starry lampshade swinging above. Since he has gone, the room hasn't been touched. Small folded T-shirts and crayons gather dust. No one is allowed to tidy or clean. For inside this room are particles of Lou, flecks of his skin and strands of his hair. Tucked in his sheets, I glance over at a mirror on the wall. Lou spent hours playing here. Eyes wide open; he plunged into a trance, frowning, grinning or opening and closing his eyes. His hand stroked the glass, an incomprehensible door.

"Hello," I remember him saying, "Hello."

In his bed, his soft toys surround me, and I press my face into worn fur. A cocoon of fuzz: three stars from his godfather Miguel. A teddy. Two unicorns. Beside me is Lala, a small fluorescent pink rabbit that Antton won at the local fair. White stuffing leaks from a rip. Absentmindedly, I tug at this hole. Often, Lou pulled at Lala's stuffing. Now, I roll fluff between my fingertips, repeating his gestures as if Lou's movements were a dance and if I learn the steps, I'll bring him back. It is wrong but somehow right, and I cry and cannot stop.

Then I remember—must unpack. But when I open my suitcase the orange notebooks are on top. An amber pull. Turning pages, I read jumbled sentences, and a series of obituaries. During my time away, I collected announcements of death, French *notices nécrologiques,* for: Monsieur Roger Aguinet, a happily retired butcher, the much-loved Madame Louise Pennec, the beautiful Clotilde Tressier, and the erudite journalist Marie-Bernadette, devoted Ingrid, Paul the husband, Alain and Nicole. Hubert and Dominique. Karine and Ingrid. Loved. Cherished. Beloved. Never forgotten. The last name on the page is in capitals. Letters scratched in blue. They stand five centimetres tall. *LOUIS.*

When I finally admitted to Dr. Vidonne that I was keeping these notebooks, she looked at me curiously. I'd never mentioned them before because despite trusting her I was frightened she would want to read each private page. I muttered, I was always muttering with her:

"It is so difficult for me, even now, to get things to make sense. Everything blurs. Me. Lou and Antton. There is so much wreckage. Irrevocable blank spots. All this." I waved my arms in the air as I often did when I spoke, "It does not stop. But when I write in these notebooks it's different."

Dr. Vidonne said:

"Writing it down may help you to remember what came first, what came after and next." Then, she looked at me with that slow stare of hers, and whispered, almost tenderly, "Write it all down, Madame. *Write*!"

At La Place, Antton appears in the bedroom. When I sit up, the sight of his beige coat is too much. "I'm not coming with you,"

I tell him, slurring slightly. In the mirror, I catch a glimpse of myself. It is as though my face has been left out in the rain. My hair stands on end. My eyes are swollen and red. White fluff is stuck to my chin.

"I can't believe it!" Antton shouts, and then he lowers his voice. "You've only just got back and you're already playing games. I don't even know where you went with that sailor, the man from the hospital. Do you know how terribly worried I've been?"

Antton storms out and slams the bedroom door. Seconds later, he yells *"Merde!"* I hear the sound of tumbling books, and imagine the yellow and black *Série Noire* falling. An avalanche of books. A swarm of bees.

I read in my notebooks:

The word swarm designates a cloud of bees or insects. There is a general sense of a large dense throng. But in old Norse "swarm" is also connected to the word for whispering. The bees are whispering, and I cannot decipher their code.

My hands tremble, and I wish I had talked to Antton, and I hope that when he gets back I find the words. I begin to think about his school meeting, and then worry about the beige coat. It is like a bird. This fact is apparent, and I am not sure where it is flying next. I pick up another orange notebook, and with a blue biro I try to draw the trench coat's shape. The front angles of the coat stretch into vast, flapping wings. The collar rises into two horns, or eyes. It isn't clear, and my sketch is badly done, but I am trying to depict the coat as a gigantic bird.

This beige bird, I suspect, is linked to Lou's death. But Lou is not the only one, there are other names, everything is connected and I will write to my local magistrate. There is a list, and it will form part of the case condemning the coat, not Antton, but the power leading the beige.

For a while, I have realised people think I am going crazy, so methodically I have prepared my case, documenting my theory with hard facts, ascertaining what is behind the plot.

Closing my eyes, I think I will explain everything to Antton later, but when I push my nose into the duvet, I catch my *buba*'s scent. For a happy moment, I inhale Lou's little boy smell, and everything returns...

It all began nine months ago, last September. Before, everything was different. Two hundred and thirty-seven days ago, my world spun, rolled, and crumbled. It is like a pregnancy wound backwards. Before that I was a language teacher, a reader, a lover, and a mother.

Back in Monsieur Kassar's school, the Centre Via Langues, I taught English to students from all walks of life: tourism, business, medical, and literary. It was a way to make a living, and I wrote on paperboards and led conversations, explaining the difference between the phrasal verbs "getting on" and "getting off." Each week, Monsieur Kassar, an amateur poet, placed a single rose in a vase on his desk, "in memory of the Lebanese Bekaa valley of my childhood where thousands of roses are grown each year."

"You're sentimental," his wife complained.

"I am romantic," he replied. "We are symbolic animals. We need metaphor."

When I finished work, at home, I played dinosaurs with Lou, moving plastic models from sofa to floor. Some evenings, Antton and I discussed future renovations for La Place, for everything was unfinished, needed re-wiring, and tiles fell from the roof. But "It will be done when we have time." We threw our hands up into the air because "*que sera.*" Instead, I read Duras in bed, and when the dawn lit the garden at La Place, I had sex with Antton. Days began and ended and, for six years, time turned that way.

Then, nine months ago, Louis went.

We were unhinged from the axis of the earth. A creak of tangled iron. A groaning fall. But perhaps the beginning is elsewhere.

Maybe we could draw the starting line at the moment Yann (the boatman) and I met, the day I arrived at the hospital, or four months later, when we climbed over the wall. That June night when we left, I barely knew Yann, but it felt like a lifetime had passed between us, as though we'd been young and grown old beneath the moon. Golden light fell into darkness, and we went to meet death and tried to journey to the end. At least, I think that is what we were doing, for I am still trying to understand. It was the journey of a mother (me) refusing to abandon her child. Alone in the underworld. Alone in a non-world. I was a woman who had lost time, who went to look for the end of time. At the start of time, I found something else.

Or...

Maybe everything began the August day our son was born, and we chose his name. For a name can be a fresh beginning, and we wanted a name that started anew. We wrote down names for both girls and boys: *James,* British names, *Marguerite,* French names, *Hannah,* Jewish names. *Arrosa,* Basque names, *Pierre,* classic names, names of poets, writers, and philosophers. Finally, we chose Louis, as it suited our baby, and the pronunciation was similar in English and French. From that day on, we called our son: Lou, Louba, little Lou, mostly I called him *buba.*

But, after his death, I wanted Antton and I to be the only ones allowed to pronounce his name: the soft "L" followed by the voiced OU and the unvoiced IS. *Louis.* In silence, my lips say his name, and I call him: *Louis.*

Or...

The beginning could be the once-upon-a-time summer day I met Antton, when I was working on the ferries. The ship sailed across the deepest part of the Channel. A red line tracked our path on a TV screen. Without this meeting, our son could not have been born. A child demands a name, a place, and a destiny.

That eighteenth summer I began to equate liberty with water and got to know the sea. To start my first job, I had travelled down from London. A turn on a coast road revealed a vista, a vast blue-green. Water moved as far as the eye could see. Fourteen years ago, something rose inside me a bit like a fighting energy. Winds spilled across the surface. Tides rose and fell. Water also forms this story. There is a surface and a deep. Froth and abyss. Water has currents. It pushes and pulls our boats.

Or...

We could go back earlier, to a linguistic initiation, when I was five, and my mum paid our neighbour Betty to teach me French, sparking off my love for the *langue française*. I learnt the lyrics to the song "Alouette" and sang about larks plucked from wing to tail. French became my second language, unlocked another world. And later, that morning bird flew me from suburbia across the sky to the ferries and Antton, to the other side of the Channel. In France, I spoke and translated birth and death. Louis and I lived and died in two languages. *Gentille alouette.* Kind lark.

Or...

I could start with my roots, dig into the past, the clay, my land, my geology, the scraps and clutter of my origins, my absent English Christian father, my omnipresent Jewish mum, Helen, Aunty Deb, my stepfather, Cyril. My family. Floating around is what they also call "the gift" which I still can't grasp.

Sometimes, it feels like a river runs fast through my veins, and I must follow its course. Is the gift the fact that until last year I was never scared? Aunty Deb called me a "plucky kid," because I was headstrong and once slapped the school bully for calling my best friend, Rachel, a "Paki." Or is the gift my solitary, awkward character? Because since I was small, I don't fit-into-the-crowd, can be charming or haunted by a black dog, a sullen fury. The "gift" was bestowed on Aunty Deb and her mother, my great-great-grandmother, who in 1912 foretold her own death on the Titanic.

My friend Dr. Rachel says superstition is all in the mind. She told me, "It's just the brain taking a break. A recent study in Helsinki showed that sceptics possess greater powers of cognitive inhibition. They have the ability to reject superstitious impulses." According to neuroscience, giving meaning to randomness is the easy way out, the basic reaction. Yet, the water inside me does not stop trying to reach out and find the answer.

For the past few months, I've written about this in the orange notebooks. Pages and pages trying to find the start. But what are beginnings? Shifting, treacherous things. It is like trying to identify the movement between silence and sound. Lou took piano lessons, pressed small fingers on the keys, and I tried to see when sound emerged or went. It was almost impossible. Beginnings are harder to pinpoint than ends. Full stops are a sign to show where a sentence is completed.

"Read to the end," Lou always said when we had stories at bedtime and it got too late, "Don't stop in the middle, Mama. Not the middle. Get to the end."

In his room, it strikes me I need to finish the story. Put the parts of Lou together before it is too late. A Roman philosopher believed that after death there is a scattering of the union. This scattering is forgetting. Things get washed away. I must gather everything I have written in the orange notebooks. Lou cannot be left stuck in the middle. These thoughts sound like a pulsar. A rapid breathless beat.

An urgent plan emerges from the crack in the ceiling, the lavender, old books, and the nectar-drunk bees. Recently, I read that 9 percent of European bees are threatened with extinction. A red list has been made. Things have happened to the bees: *habitat loss, pesticides and fertilizers, urban development, and climate change.* Things are getting lost. Bees and boys.

Frowning, I write in the orange notebook:

1. *Assemble Lou. Every memory, recollection.*
2. *Explain the journey I have been on. What I've understood.*
3. *Tell Lou his story. My story. The story of Antton and I. Tell him the things I never got a chance to say.*

I must put Lou in the right burning place in my heart, for my baby wanders; he haunts me, day and night. Sometimes, I feel his small hands clinging to my legs, and his grip stops me from advancing. He is calling me. Yann heard him too. Antton may have caught Lou's whispers, but we couldn't talk about this. It was a pain that hurt too much if we went too near.

Lou is lost, and our little *buba* is adrift. He roams between worlds unable to find his way home. Lou should have lost his milk teeth, finished childhood, become a teenager, grown into an adult. He should have, I have said to myself so many times, because "should have" is a conditional tense, expressing a past expectation that was not met. I taught this to students, wrote on a blackboard:

We use "should have" to describe a situation with regret, where we wish to go back in time and transform an event. A "should have" clause is often followed with a BUT.

Lou should have been here BUT he is dead. Death is definitive.

Death will be definitive. The grammar tense does not change.

Yet, I wrote in the notebooks:

Orpheus went down into Hades to get his dead wife, sang songs charming the underworld. He did the impossible: wept 247 litres of tears. Used 350 boxes of Kleenex bought in bulk. He spent sleepless nights reading thousands of self-help books. Orpheus implored to a gaggle of Olympian gods, who told him grief had five stages he should accept. But Orpheus couldn't follow that path. "I mean," he told them, "I can't erase my wife's photos from my timeline. She's been there for 2,000 years." Instead, he dared to pass through the Gates of Tenaro, and the dark torrents of Styx to reach the place of the dead.

As for me, I've read the book, got the T-shirt, seen the movie, and re-told the story. I am a mother with a dead child. A not-mother, stuck between worlds.

I am writing these notebooks. All of it is here, even if my psychiatrist said, "There are memories we'll never recall, and our memories of things can change. It is a healthy process for everything we have known to evolve. The present affects the way we understand the past. Memories are living things." Dr. Vidonne used the word *"vivante,"* which means "living" in French. The opening "vee" sound feels buoyant and fresh. On the periodic table, V is the symbol for vanadium, turning certain emeralds a milky-green. Green is a sign of life. In the lush Basque valleys, the word for life is *bizitza,* pronounced bee-zitz-ah.

When I have finished writing, I will try and get the notebooks to Lou, I can teach him languages, about bees and the chromatic wheel. If he is growing up somewhere, he can read this when he is ten, eighteen, or thirty-four. He can flip through these notebook pages in his forties or fifties. He will be older than me.

Snuggling under the covers, I glance at myself a final time in the mirror.

I forget to take off my sunglasses and fall asleep thinking about bees.

1a. A Glory

Cherries. Vanilla ice cream, Sprinkles. Everything—these were the ingredients of your favourite dessert, an ice-cream sundae that you called a "Glory." We made Glories for your birthday every year. The tradition started when you were one. My mum, your Nana Helen, sent the recipe by email for her Best Grandson's Birthday.

Special Knickerbocker Glory Recipe for my Best Grandson's Birthday

Get many tall glasses. Pretty as possible. Put cherries at the bottom (these are the treasure & you get them last). Put a layer of tinned mixed fruit (more colours the better). Then, a scoop of vanilla ice cream. Cover with a layer of sprinkled nuts & raspberry sauce. Put another layer of fruit, ice cream, nuts & sauce. Repeat, giggling, until the glass is full. Squeeze cream on top. Decorate the Knickerbocker with sprinkles. Put a candle on top. Light it. Sing happy birthday to the best grandson. Blow it out and make a wish.

Buba, on your very last birthday, you were six. We were on holiday on the Riviera, and prepared the Glories together, put sprinkles and sauce on the top. "*C'est* delish," you announced in *franglais*, ice cream smeared around your mouth.

My temporal arrow has been reduced to ash. It is the plainest horror, *buba*, never to see you again. On your birthday, this year, I will eat ice cream and celebrate you. Happy birthday. Make a wish. Blow out the light.

2. Two Sides of a Mirror

When I left the hospital with Yann (the boatman) to go on the journey, we had one small bag each, and we climbed over a wall. There are certain key instants in life that we are blind to; we walk nonchalantly as empires tumble and don't notice when fortunes progress. But that evening I weighed the gravity of outcomes and felt change as if it were a ticking bomb. Despite the heat, I shivered, worrying about what was ahead. Yann handed me his sweatshirt. I pulled it over my clothes, and he said, "We are doing the right thing."

Yet, we could have left the hospital differently, and I realise that now, for no one was forcing us to stay. We could have told everyone and left in broad daylight. But Yann insisted, "Climbing over something has been the best idea since Caesar stepped over the Rubicon. Afterwards, you can't turn back."

It was August when I encountered Antton (your papa) on the ferry. I was eighteen and, without Rachel, nothing would have occurred. Sometimes, I wonder if Rachel understands that without the newspaper advert that she thrust in my hand, *buba*, you would not have been born.

"Look! *Wanted Hostesses FeelBright Ferries. Fluent French required,*" she shouted.

My bedroom door opened, "Work hard. A-level exams soon!" My stepfather Cyril's pale round face peeked in.

"Of course," I answered, mouthing to Rachel, "I hate him." Two years ago, Cyril had married my mum and moved into my home. My anger at him knew no bounds. Every day, I fantasised about volcanic fights with him, and often I provoked them. "I can't wait to get out of here." I rolled my eyes and Rachel sighed.

Downstairs in the freshly painted hall was Cyril's Meccano Ferris wheel. The day he'd arrived, he'd removed our seaside photos, and the charcoal caricature of Aunty Deb, my mum, and me, done cheap by a Covent Garden artist. In their place, the Ferris wheel was assembled from coloured metal strips and tiny bolts. It was as tall as me, and regularly polished and maintained.

Cyril told visitors proudly, "I used two kits to build the double counter-rotating wheel. It took six months." Little model passengers were placed in each seat: families with children, couples holding hands, an old beret-wearing lady with a basket and a cat. There were people of colour, a fireman, a policewoman, and an Orthodox Jew in a big black hat. "I had them made especially." Cyril smiled and rocked on the balls of his feet, and I was embarrassed when his plump body swayed. The wheel was fully operational and on special occasions, Cyril put on the lights.

"Stop drifting off and do my hair and I'll write your application letter for the ferry!" Rachel handed me a hairbrush. On the bed, we curled into each other as I got the knots out of her thick black locks. In this friendship, our boundaries came and went. "Laurel and Hardy," the mean girls called us at the grammar school. She: an Anglo-Iranian. "Fat" (the mean girls said), a Rubenesque beauty made from curves (I thought). Me: a small and skinny Anglo-Jew. "A fucking midget," the mean girls said. "Stylish and mysterious," Rachel told me, "especially with your glorious hair."

Both of us came from mixed marriages, her middle name was Anna, and mine—Rachel. "It's an incredible coincidence," we said, astounded by the rarity of our connections. In my bedroom, her big body held my tiny one as she scribbled. We talked about school, my favourite books, being feminists, chip butties (ketchup or brown sauce?), Rachel's fling with the handsome son of the local greengrocer, going to university in the autumn, and the new Spice Girls' song. "A zigazigaaaaaa?" Rachel mocked. She was my best and only friend.

She typed:

Dear Sir/Madam,

Regarding your recent advert, I am applying to be a Hostess For Feelbright Ferries. I have experience in the service industry.

It was a lie.

"Let's make it up," Rachel said because she always thought big. Her mum, who was a doctor, (and had grown up between Tehran and London) read self-help books about *Thinking Outside the Box* and *Stepping Outside of Who You Think You Are.* We did. In my bedroom, Rachel and I conjured up an irreproachable Anna Nelson, the surname I had got from the dad I had barely met. In our imaginary world I had:

Three years' experience as a kitchen aide. Two years' experience running summer camps. We wrote: *I am dynamic, hardworking and have good people skills.* In reality, I was uncomfortable in crowds, liked nothing better than spending the day under my duvet, eating Maltesers, discovering what Rachel called my "gina," having my first orgasms, and reading books. Occasionally I went on my own to the Barbican Centre and watched dream-like surrealist French films where couples drove around country lanes lying beneath sheets in fantasy cars like double beds. We wrote: *I speak fluent French, and enjoy reading...* and I was relieved we had added something true. For books belonged to me and since I was a child I read so much I wasn't always sure whether a memory belonged to me or had happened on the page.

The day I met Yann I was falling apart. It was February and everything had come undone. It was very different circumstances to when I met your papa. For the first time in my life, I was consumed with fear. It ran inside me, inconsolable. My insomnia was out of control. Dr. Vidonne had prescribed "rest."

On a wet, winter day, an ambulance drove me through hospital gates. The grounds were spotted with buildings, some low-lying and others tall. Trees sprang up against the sky. The bare branches were like a web, and I was not sure whether I had been caught or saved. For a net can prevent the death of an acrobat or cage a wild animal.

Welcome to the Hôpital Psychiatrique du Val, the sign above the door said, and Antton and I walked inside. In a consulting room, a dark-haired female nurse with tired eyes handed me a form, and I trembled when she instructed, "Please sign here." Antton stayed as I took off my clothes and put on hospital pyjamas. The nurse informed me, "You're in the closed ward now. But in a week or so, with Dr. Vidonne's authorisation, we can move you to an open ward." I nodded as she led me to the corridor and told Antton and me, "It is time to say goodbye."

We held each other, and he ran his fingers over my recently cut, short hair, whispering, "*Je t'aime.* Take care. You'll be home soon." He seemed flustered, and I wondered why Antton wasn't relieved. I was lost, but now he could go home, get strong. His cheekbones cut sharp in his face. In the corridor, he had tears in his eyes, but I didn't cry. The dark-haired nurse glanced at her watch, and suddenly Antton was gone. The ward door locked behind him.

Nearby, men and women ambled and mumbled. A man swayed back and forth, occasionally shrieking a high-pitched "fuck." Through a barred window, I saw huddles of patients smoke roll-ups in the rain. Two nurses in white uniforms stopped and said, "Hello." Somewhere a man began screaming.

An alarm went off. The nurses ran, including the dark-haired one. A woman sidled up to me, in a smart green dress. "Pleased to meet you. I am the Queen of France, and they are holding me here against my will. It is terrible as I am pregnant with triplets." Shocked, I ignored her, and she walked away grumbling about the guillotine. Then, she came back and offered me a toffee which I accepted. As I put the sweet into my mouth, I wanted to laugh because, and I write this carefully, I suddenly felt at home, and strangely safe behind locked doors.

Eventually, the dark-haired nurse returned, explaining there had been "an emergency." She sighed and showed me to a room with white walls, a single bed, and a bedside table. As she watched, I unpacked. Then, she removed some of my things, such as a pair of nail scissors, and I understood she was concerned I might harm myself. Finally, she looked at her watch again. "Time to go! From two to four, we lock bedrooms. It's coffee time and everyone must socialise. Doctors' orders."

I found myself in a large room and, by a coffee tray, a man put out his hand for me to shake.

"*Bonjour.* My name is Yann." Ignoring him, I reached for a cup, but could only find a chipped one. The man came and whispered in my ear:

"There is a crack running through you." I turned, startled. "It is running through you, the crack reaches today. It is a strong line, and you should follow it." It felt like the man could see straight inside me. He had strawberry blond greying hair, and was wiry but muscular, heading toward fifty, but not yet there. His rolled-up shirtsleeves revealed faded dark blue tattoos, an anchor, something nautical. He could have been ex-Navy, had the rough politeness of obedience slapped into shape, and he reminded me of the ferry crew I'd known, years before: Skippers and marine engineers. Boatmen. Sailors.

I wanted to push him away, but then I noticed his pale blue eyes. They were deceptively limpid, as though he had nothing to hide. But a face without secrets is impossible, like a landscape without memory, for geology and genealogy share things. Time has a past tense.

He smiled. "A crack. Yes, yes, yes a crack."

"Please go away."

"I can't, petite Camille," he shrugged.

"My name is Anna!"

"Camille. Camille. I am Yann."

Buba, from then on, Yann refused to call me anything else. Even though I told him, over and over, my name was Anna. My mum had chosen this name and it was mine. To my complaints he replied, "People can be renamed. They are like water, once poured they can fit inside any vessel," and it seemed to make him happy calling me Camille. As though he had found an old treasure in the back of a drawer and held it up to the light. After a while, I got used to my new name. But I wonder now if I became someone else. As though the appellation gradually cast a spell. Perhaps, *buba,* I should have kept a critical objective distance from our relationship, or perhaps I was a bad influence, and Yann should have stayed away. Or maybe he was deluded, and led me astray. Possibly on that first day, by the coffee tray, I should have remained silent.

Behind me, a woman began to moan, "When am I leaving? When? When? When?"

A nurse answered her, "Madame, you'll be leaving soon." I noticed the Queen of France woman had stood up and began singing *La Marseillaise.* Smiling to myself, I thought, I had only just arrived at the hospital. This destination was the bottom of a hole, yet I was sure it was here I would find the answer to you, *buba.* Clarity would come from the hardest ground.

At four o'clock, a male nurse walked down the corridor. His keys chinked as he walked, and soon I would become accustomed to this metallic sound, locking and unlocking, the opening and the closing of doors. When I was finally allowed back inside my room, I collapsed on my bed, and fell into a deep, sudden sleep.

When I woke up, I was trembling from a dream I couldn't remember. Looking around me, I saw the white walls and, surprisingly, for the first time in weeks, I was able to calm my fears. Reaching to my bedside table, I grabbed a notebook I had brought with me, and wrote down a word that had come as I slept. The word had troubled me deeply, carried a great sense of dread. The notebook was orange, but the first word I wrote inside it was: *BEIGE*.

I wrote in the notebooks, *buba,* sentences beginning in the hospital on the very first day. In my room, I wondered about truth, like I had when we wrote the application letter, when Rachel re-invented Anna Nelson, made me into someone else. When you died, I no longer knew who I was. What mattered? My moral compass veered. My dilemmas about freedom vanished, and the decisions, debates, the small white lies. My interest in idle gossip dissolved. Even my belief in goodness failed. When you went, I wrote sentences about how I was no longer sure about kindness. I wrote sentences about the awfulness of the world, a place where anything could happen at any time. A sentence is also a judgement. A sentence is final, and it has an end.

In the hospital, Yann gave me a piece of paper, and on it was written:

We die every day, more or less, simply and purely, absolutely, without precision. There are no big deaths or little deaths. Just death.

In our Edgware kitchen, my mum was squeezing teabags, sliding hot brown pillows onto a small cream china dish—bought by Cyril to avoid "nasty drips." She shook her head when she saw my crumpled anarchist T-shirt. Recently, my mum had been shaking her head at me from morning until night. We were both uncomfortable with our growing conflicts. She liked dresses. I wore trousers. She was tall. I was short. I read from dawn till dusk and she never opened a book. But until now we had relished these differences. It was as though we were magnets and what had been our opposite poles of attraction had become repulsions.

"What do you want for breakfast?" She stood up, suddenly, bright as a bird. "You must eat. Build up your strength. Eggs, cereal, toast. I could do you a bagel with salmon and cream cheese? Rachel told me you have applied for a job."

The fridge hummed, filled to the brim with a cheese selection (in a plastic box), tubs of chopped herring, hummus, coleslaw, potato salad, and plastic-wrapped piles of latkes. A jelly set with strawberries inside. A melon. A roasting chicken. Pickles in a glass jar. Mayonnaise. Ketchup. Sandwich spread. Skimmed milk for Cyril who had cholesterol. Low-sugar diabetic jam. Brown sauce to be served with fried fish, slathered on white bread. Three cartons of cheap juice. A sealed jar of olives I'd brought back from a school trip to France. I was starving and furious at Rachel for talking to my mum.

"So," my mum crouched, peering into the fridge, "what do you fancy?"

"I'm not hungry," I lied, knowing it would hurt her.

Her face fell, lit by the fridge light's glow. She went and opened a kitchen cabinet, reached for a bottle of pills. "Just to calm my nerves," she said to no one.

"I'm going to have a shower," I snapped. She'd been popping pills for years.

A French philosopher wrote that becoming mobilises the impossible.

The summer of my eighteenth birthday, I examined my reflection in my bedroom mirror: I thought the ferry job would be an escape route from my face, from where I was, from my once-home, and our row of measly houses on the outskirts of London. On the underground network, we were the final stop. You had to be patient when you took the train. "Mind the gap," the recorded voice said when the doors slid open. That year, I wanted to run. I didn't know I would meet Antton. Your papa. Meet your beginning. That summer, I ran toward the sea.

Homes, bees, and hearts:

Some bees nest in the ground and others in trees. When looking upwards, some bees excavate in plants, and others in rock crevices or abandoned nests. Some species nest exclusively in empty snail shells. The ground-nesting species make up over half of all the bees in the world. Exposure and a degree of slope influence their choice of home.

I wonder about this: when do we make a home? How do we make a home? Why do we make a home? The Romans carried their home gods' statues, the Penates, with them when they travelled, always keeping their home close.

They say home is where the heart is. Bees have hearts with eight chambers. A human heart has four chambers. A chamber is a room. Whether we are a bee or a human being, we always need an opening, an entrance, a window, or a door so other people can enter. The spaces we love are unwilling to remain permanently closed. Buba, where is the key to the door that I can unlock to let you in?

When I met Yann I was falling apart. It was a different day to when I met Antton. The two meetings are pillars in the building of my story. It is not what I expected, Lou, to tell you these dual tales. It is as though they are side mirrors on a dressing table. I am in the middle and they face each other. Antton and Yann. Two different men. Two opposites of the looking glass. One arrived in my life before your birth, the other after your death. When I arrived at the hospital it was with Antton, and I left with Yann. Which one is real, which is not? Your death stands between them. It is holding their hands.

You never met Yann, but I wish you had. Many times, I told him about you, when we walked in the hospital grounds, tramping through winter and the spring. In the cold sunshine, mist, and rain, I told him things I had never told anyone: that after you died "it was impossible to move on, for my future guillotined Lou's future." I talked to him about the flashbacks when they first came. "I couldn't speak that day. The words were stuck in my throat." With Yann, I talked freely, the way we can with a stranger. The way we talk to someone we might never see again. The way we talk when we could lie and invent stuff (for the other person can't verify the facts) and yet we choose honesty. The company of strangers is a remarkable space for truth.

I remember this:

The last time we were in London, Antton lifted you up, and I placed your six-year-old finger in the centre of the Tube map, moved it out along the thick black line past Euston, northwest until we reached our destination. "Here is where I grew up. My home. The last stop on the Northern Line. Edgware." Your finger touched a black bar at the end of the line.

Later, we walked out of Edgware Station into a wall of heat. For years, I had fled, but I kept coming back. A band of yellow pollution stained the sky. On the pavement was the latest edition of Metro. Newspaper headlines: *Knife Attacks on Increase.* Rival gangs under sixteen, and twelve. Cabs waited for customers. Burly white men in black leather jackets consulted their phones. "The only thing Edgware is famous for is Dick Turpin, the highwayman. He set fire to a farmer and raped a girl here," my stepfather had once said. Your father's nose wrinkled at the scent of melting tar, cheap perfume, sweat, and car fumes. "It's nothing like La Place. How did you choose to make a home somewhere so different from where you grew up?"

La Place became our home. We made it somehow, the three of us. The word "home" comes from the Old English ham, meaning a village where many souls are gathered. A home is shelter. In French, the word "home" does not exist. We say "la maison," "chez soi" or "le foyer." The old-fashioned latter word is what I prefer, "le foyer" is the hearth, the centre of things. The word "foyer" is linked to another word: focus. A home is a concentration of light.

Buba, if we put all these etymologies and meanings together, we could say: A home is a shelter where our gathered souls shine.

"We're here. In Edgware!" Your little fingers clasped mine, and we walked down Station Road, Antton beside us, shoulders hunched. "Will we see Nana soon?" I squeezed your hand.

"Soon, my *buba*." Your eyes took in the Pound stores selling: mops, torches, notebooks, Mars bars, deodorant, Sellotape. Three rolls for a pound. Inside shop windows, dummies wore knock-off clothes, fakes and discards. Deal after deal. "Look! You can get your eyebrows threaded for a tenner." Antton frowned and I felt cross, because he didn't like the street or the area. I wanted to tell him he could collect beauty from the gutter and stars, from trash and cathedrals, wastebins and books. In my mind, I wrote lists of languages and shops: 1) *Turkish,*

Gujarati, Persian, Romanian, Yiddish, English, Hindu, and more. 2) *Gold shops. Starbucks, where five black and white girls in cheap tracksuits share two lattes. Charity shops. Money transfers. Halal and kosher butchers. Let the blood drip a different way. Phone shops. Betting shops.* Antton pulled himself inward, a Basque man from the mountains, the summits reaching pure air. As he recoiled I relished sticky pavements and crowds. Here in Edgware, *buba*, your papa and I didn't fit. I wanted him to love Greens 24/7 World Supermarket where I bought freshly baked pita, Polish pickles, packets of freekeh piled next to fridges with thirty types of feta, bundles of okra, and Turkish Kaymak cream. I wished he enjoyed the Jewish bakeries, selling bagels by the dozen, boiled or baked. All closed on Saturdays. Open on Sundays. But he did savour the food from the Indian take-away, whose owner set off fireworks at Diwali, keeping everyone awake. Even Antton understood, spice and beauty must invade the night.

Philosophers write that even if the stars stopped turning, and with them, all the clocks in the universe, and even if the years and the seasons fell into oblivion, time would keep flowing.

Buba, since you have gone, I am not sure...

At the front door, we didn't need to knock. My mum flung it open, dragged us in. "Like an octopus," Antton commented later, as though multiple arms drew us close.

"Lou! You're so handsome!" my mum screamed with delight. Squeezing your cheeks, she asked question after question, "Was the boat busy? Was the Tube busy? Why didn't we bring our car? How was work at the language school? Earning enough money? How was the house, La Place? What a funny name. Have you mended the roof? Any problems? Was I pregnant? Would we have another child? Shouldn't wait too long. Would we like tea? Water? Coffee? Wine? Food?" She looked at Antton. He hunched his shoulders. Her questions were like needles, unashamedly pushing through barriers. Yet, finally, her threads held us together, and we were stitched into the story she made of our family. Sewn into a life.

When I met Yann, everything was tumbling. I repeat myself, because he noticed the crack, yet in the place of disaster, he saw a path. It was like the fissure in your bedroom ceiling, *buba,* it led to the lampshade and the stars; the crack reached the firmament. It was spreading, and its shape was dendritic, dividing into branches. The word dendritic begins with a D, a letter that also contains a curl. The crack inside me didn't seem to stop.

But Yann and I met on the inside, on what Yann called "the other side" in a psychiatric hospital. Do you think I cracked under the pressure, lost the plot, lost my mind? To think I had lost something, as though sanity could be mislaid like a sock or a son. As though reason was a possession one parted with by mistake. It was what I had taught medical students during my lessons at the Centre Via Langues, writing idiomatic expressions with a blue marker:

To lose yourself, to lose your cool, to lose contact, to lose your mind. To lose your marbles, to lose your head, to lose the thread.

When you went, I was struck by the force of being with the dead. I heard this force in the mouths of other mothers with lost children. It felt like I lost everything.

Yann came to see me later that first day. He knocked on my door, and before I could answer, he entered, speaking loudly, "Bonjour Camille. Please let me introduce myself again. My name is Yann." He smiled. Trembling, I watched him stride to the window. My chest felt tight like I couldn't breathe, I clutched the notebook and at first was too surprised to speak. Then I asked him, "Please could you go. I need to rest."

"It's such a quiet evening." He ignored what I'd said. "If you like I can show you around the hospital. I've been here a few times. This time I won't stay for long. I promised myself I'd get back to work. I've left my car parked nearby. I can see it from here."

He pointed, and Yann stood, steady as a rock. But my mind was blurred with thoughts of beige. There was fog in front of everything and I could just make out forms, and yet, when I tried to look at them they disappeared. Yann barely moved, and it felt like he had always been there, in that spot in my room, lost in the darkening sky. "I need to get back to work," he repeated. I shoved the notebook under my pillow, scared that he might steal it and, shaking, I asked again,

"Please leave my room. Please leave my room!"

With his back to me, Yann said, "Petite Camille, look at the crack. You have to look at the crack."

I began shouting then, I couldn't stop myself.

"PLEASE leave my room. PLEASE leave my room. LEAVE MY ROOM!"

A nurse arrived and told Yann to get out, and he left without glancing back.

Relieved, I reached beneath my pillow. My hands shook as I held the orange notebook close to my heart. Opening the pages, I returned to the word BEIGE and, counting the five letters, I wondered at their significance. An interest in numbers had come to me from Aunty Deb, a numerology devotee via the Kabbalah.

"We have been counting things since the first humans made scratch marks on bones to show the cycles of the moon," she claimed, persuading me to count the pink geraniums on her balcony, magpies, the honey poured into her cake, the Passover biscuits she baked by the dozen, for "Pythagoras thought even numbers were female and odd numbers were male."

When I was a child, Aunty Deb gave me a book about numbers and bees, and inside it was written:

During its first three days of life, a bee eats approximately 3,000 meals.

By the sixth day, a growing bee has multiplied its initial weight by 500.

It requires 556 worker bees to gather a pound of honey.

Bees fly more than once around the world to gather a pound of honey.

The average life of a honeybee during the working season is about six weeks.

Buba, when you began to learn maths at school, you asked me one day:

"What would it be like if number one was the biggest number, and the smallest number was a million billion zillion. Imagine if a million billion zillion was at the beginning and the number one was at the end?"

The most important thing humans count is time. We count minutes, hours, years, and centuries, seasons, lives, and the creation of earth. We make schedules, mark anniversaries, refer to the present, future, and past. Many of us know that the true time, the real temporal revolution, is not the turning of the planets, the clocks, or the seconds flickering on a stopwatch. Real time is an intimate, elastic thing. But you knew something completely different, my *buba*. You knew that life could be lived backwards.

My summer job application was successful. I left home to be a hostess for Feelbright Ferries. The night before boarding, I stayed at Aunty Deb's coastal council flat. She'd moved out of London to be near the sea, what she called, quoting Wordsworth, "A mighty harmonist."

Opening the door, she shrieked, "Darling!" and hugged me. Her head reached my shoulder. Dark curls tickled my nose. My Aunty Deb was almost as wide as she was short. Over her purple polka dot top, her red skirt rode high beneath her breasts. "You look gorgeous." Her kiss left a scarlet smear.

"I've just won fifty quid at the races. The horse was called Bonne Chance." She told me to put my suitcase down, that I should eat, that I was skinny, clever, strange, and should cut my hair, dye it, or get it straightened with a Brazilian treatment. She had a neighbour who could do it cheap. Aunty Deb liked betting, had never married, and had once been a Communist. Cyril described her as "difficult." In a rare moment of rebellion, my mum replied, "Stop. She's a good woman." For Aunty Deb had often waded fearlessly into the river of our days, bringing stories, cash, and cake.

Over tea, served in floral bone china, Aunty Deb read my palm. "You'll meet a handsome man. Just like Lady Di. Did you know she's dating Dodi the Egyptian billionaire?" she sighed, and I sighed. We loved Lady Di. "My friend Harold is a tailor, and he had to make the whole Egyptian billionaire family, including Dodi, velvet tracksuits." She served me a slice of dark brown cake "made with honey given to me by a beekeeper who lives at the end of a lane." She winked but I wasn't sure why, and then began to talk about her "gift," which meant she always got the good honey. My mum didn't like it when Aunty Deb mentioned this "gift." "Just silly superstition. Nothing but a load of malarkey."

"Eat your cake." Aunty Deb bit into her slice. "Delicious honey."

Making honey:

Less than 4 percent of all bee species make honey. Studies show that exposure to neonicotinoid pesticides leads directly to the loss of honeybees.

Honey is made from the nectar carried by honeybees. When their nectar sacks are full, honeybees return to the hive and deliver the nectar to indoor bees, passing it mouth-to-mouth, from bee to bee, until its moisture content is reduced. This changes the nectar into honey.

Buba, it is strange to think that honey has been inside bees' mouths.

Buba, have you spoken to the bees?

"What do you really mean by this gift?" I asked Aunty Deb later, as we ate turkey sausages, boiled potatoes and peas.

"It's just following your nose. Intuition." She squirted a shiny mahogany puddle of brown sauce onto her plate. "You know it saved my life when the Nazis came. All my family was taken. It was only by chance I was saved..." There was a long pause and Aunty Deb spoke again: "Mostly, the gift is about listening to your dreams." She repeated the word "dream" as she stirred her tea, drawing circles with her spoon until a small vortex turned.

That day, I wanted to ask her more questions, *buba*: which dreams I should listen to, those from the day or from the night? I had always been a bad sleeper, but when I was eighteen, my insomnia got worse. Fuzzy from fatigue, I imagined things in the daytime. As her spoon hit china, I longed to know, should I hear and see those dreams that fell into my mind when I was on the tube and pictured the train upside down and all the passengers floating, dressed in city suits and saris? Or should I listen to the dreams where I argued with Cyril, where wars were fought and tiny iridescent reptiles crawled over ancient battlegrounds? Which dreams were important?

I didn't get a chance to ask her, as Deb's telephone rang, and she began talking about Lady Diana and Saint-Tropez, the Retired Roller-skating Club, and her new "friend," a Spanish woman, a widow who'd owned a hair-dressing salon. They were flying to Torremolinos for the weekend for a baby shower.

The following morning, before I left to start my new job, Aunty Deb gave me five slices of honey cake triple-wrapped in film, double-wrapped in tin foil, and sealed inside a zip-lock plastic bag. She pushed fifty pounds into my pocket and cried.

"I'm just being silly." She enveloped me in a hug so tight I could barely breathe. It was years before I saw my Aunty Deb again.

On the ferries shifts started at 5:00 a.m., sometimes drifted on until midnight. The boat was registered on the Cayman Islands. A million miles away on a *paradis fiscal*. I didn't know what a tax haven was, and I pictured an island in the Caribbean where palm trees grew, and I lay beneath their fronds, a volume of Rimbaud's poetry in my hand, reading about the rising of fresh harmony. Innocence was my middle name.

During my first days, at the port, before embarkation, I walked down a slipway, and when no one was looking I dipped my fingers in the sea. One by one, I placed each finger in my mouth. The salty water was sweet and burnt my tongue. This job was different from anything I'd done before. The water became an anchor.

The night I met your papa, I'd been working on the ferries for a month. I was behind a curtain separating first class from second. The fabric was itchy but allowed me to hide from my supervisor, and my job. While we had lied on my application letter, on the ferry my lack of experience was telling.

Ignoring customers, I spent too long staring out of portholes. On a rough crossing, I dropped ketchup onto a seated bald man's head. The red sauce dripped into a line of scarlet circles that made me think of Plato and his perfect forms. The man shouted, "Bloody hell. Get me your manager!"

"You better pull your socks up," my supervisor said, and I replied:

"I am following regulations and not wearing socks but tights."

She raised her eyebrows, gave me a warning, and, afterwards, I cried. It was the first time I had been away from home. I missed my mum and my morning cup of tea in bed. "You need me," the tea carried by her hand explained. "We need each other," my mum and I had always said. We had often shared a bed, for even as a child, my sleep had been precarious, nighttime ghosts and monsters invading my sleep. My mum's arms held me as I navigated mansion houses with speaking fireplaces and children made from wicker. "It's just a dream," she would tell me when I woke sobbing from a nightmare where eyes stared at me from the darkness.

For sixteen years we lived alone. She cooked, and I learnt to mend things, unblock toilets, and paint walls. I had hung the pictures in the hallway, and when he arrived Cyril took them down and put his wheel there instead.

On the ferry, I was pulling back the curtain, when Antton stepped on my toe.

"*Ça va*?" he said when I stumbled. Those were his first words, or at least I think they were. We were in the middle of the Channel. The sea was rough, and the boat jolted on the swell. Steadying myself, I looked into his eyes. I recall that first look. Brown eyes and thick black lashes. He wore a navy-blue polo neck and above it his face turned green. "*Ça va*?" he repeated. The boat jolted again and before I could answer, Antton vomited on the floor. Luckily, I wasn't squeamish, and I patted his back and said, in French:

"Please sit down, sir," as I had been taught to do during our training on customer care. He was wearing beige trousers, cotton chinos. The beige trench coat was beside him.

It has been a worrying discovery, as I write, that the colour beige and the trench coat were present at this moment. The start of your destiny. Even in the days beforehand, there was beige when I left Edgware. Beige walls, carpet, fittings, and trimmings. The kitchen surfaces and the background to the Ferris wheel. Then, when Antton and I met, beige was a stubborn fact. If we scanned this precise instant for beige, the screen would glow infrared. Alarm bells would ring, sirens wail. Antton's coat was cream, almost cappuccino. His trousers pale brown. A smothering shade. It is a clue in the unravelling of this plot: *BEIGE,* the five letters at the start of the orange notebook.

Researchers, poets, painters, and fools have all written about the history of colours. Antton taught a *lycée* class on chromatic theory. At La Place, he grabbed books from our shelves and read passages out loud:

"Look, colour meanings are constructed by culture and history. They spin like the chromatic wheel. Yellow has been used to identify treachery, Renaissance prostitutes, and Jews."

"Like myself," I interjected, and he nodded. "But it is also the colour of radiating gold. Green was considered unlucky to take on boats. To wear on stage. Green, a painter says, is a good warm light. Yet, it can also mean growth, and as for red." Antton paused dramatically, as I knew he did in front of his students, and held his hands in a practised pose:

"Red is ambiguous. In recent Western history, it has become our sign of danger: stop signs, poison, fire, sex. But red was worn for European mediaeval weddings. In China, it symbolises good luck." Antton explained blue, black, white, orange, and pink. But he did not understand colours are puzzles, or at least he never said, and I wrote in the notebooks:

Colours are not possessions, but intimate revelations of energy. They are light waves with mathematical lengths.

Spectrophotometers measure their curves; they calculate their dance. Colours are resonant mysteries.

That first evening dusk fell, and through my window I saw the black tracery sway, trees creaked in sudden gusts and blows. The locals said the wind "came down from the mountains." It was unpredictable. As the sky grew dark, something strange began to happen, and I put on my sunglasses and began to write, consumed by an energy I had not felt since you'd left.

For weeks, at La Place, I had stayed in bed, or slumped on the sofa. I stopped reading and didn't eat. Instead, I drank wine, sang lullabies, and watched television: quiz shows, murder series, and lengthy documentaries on climate change. Things on the screen were far-away-out-of-reach. During sleepless nights, I heard each creak and crack, checked the locks on each door.

But on that hospital evening, warmth spread through me. As I wrote, the vitality from my lost days returned. Tension faded, and inertia became liveliness. My arm moved across the page and I couldn't stop, not even when a short, plump nurse popped her head around the door:

"*Bonsoir, Madame.* Hurry up, it's dinnertime. It's obligatory to eat together in the refectory."

When I told her I couldn't, she frowned and wrote something down.

"As it's the first night, you can eat in your room. But afterwards you'll have to join the other patients. Those are Dr. Vidonne's rules."

The nurse returned with a dinner tray with a starter of diced purple beetroot in vinaigrette, turkey escalope in a cream sauce with rice, a piece of Camembert cheese and a crème caramel. She watched me as I ate, and I moved the food until the sauces mixed and everything became a violent pink.

"Not hungry?" The nurse looked at her watch, and then at me. "Madame, why don't you take your sunglasses off?"

"I have sensitive eyes and need to wear them because of the bright light."

She said, "But Madame it is dark outside," and I nodded. Then she wrote something else down and went away.

In the middle of the Channel, being careful to avoid his vomit, I handed the seasick man (your papa-to-be) a cup of water.

"What is your name?" I asked, following my training, which claimed customer support was improved if two individuals identify themselves.

"My name is Antton," he said, "but spelt with two Ts, as I am half-Basque." Lurching, he was sick again into a paper bag. I wondered why he was talking to me about spelling. It was only later, *buba*, I would come to know your papa's constant search for linguistic perfection, as though he was a carpenter attempting the perfect wooden angle, the smoothest join. In his quest, Antton even corrected strangers.

"I really don't like the sea. I am much happier on the land," he said.

Smiling, I replied, "I love it." We sped over the waves.

The sea was calmer now and, when I looked up at the screen suspended on the wall, I saw the red line showing our route. We were travelling over the Channel area called Portland, and Hurd's Deep. Later, I got in the habit of telling customers, "We're sailing over Hurd's Deep, the deepest part of the Channel. Beneath us, a pro-glacial chalk ridge collapsed, causing a catastrophic flood. Weapons were dumped here, nuclear waste, bombs," until my supervisor overheard me and said, "You're making people stressed."

That summer, as I ventured outside my home, I began to understand people didn't want to think about watery chasms, unforeseen areas, deep-edged trenches of danger. At Hurd's Deep plates had shifted. The result was an abyss. Enter at your peril. Sink without a trace. On the seabed inexplicable things happened.

Antton and I began to talk. If I recall correctly, I found out he taught literature in a *lycée* in Paris but hated city life and wanted to move back to the countryside.

"To the southwest, I need to return near to the mountains." He stretched out his legs as though he needed to scramble over slopes. He learnt I was from London and about to go and study French, Art, and Philosophy at Warwick University. Our conversation veered from our shared love of reading, from Baudelaire to mayonnaise (I loved it, he hated it), Louise Bourgeois, the Beatles (he was a fan, and I told him my Aunty Deb had seen them live in concert, screaming so loud she lost her voice) and back to Hannah Arendt. A question she asks still persists in my mind, it's like the question I asked after you went. The question I asked Dr. Vidonne:

How do you continue loving the world, express *amor mundi*, how do you care, in the midst of total suffering and despair?

The loss of a child is against the order of things. That is what they say in France. It brings about a state of total disarray. Arendt's question is relevant for an individual tragic death or a mass tragic killing. This question appears in the notebooks on so many pages. It seems to be at the heart of everything:

How do you keep alive and loving when your world falls apart? What do you do without religion?

Through a ferry window, I noticed the sun rising in the east. Rays lit the waves in a sudden gleam. The sky glowed pink streaked with tangerine. It was morning. Work was calling. Soon, we'd arrive in France. On the other side of the lounge,

I heard people mumbling and talking; a crowd had gathered round the wall-mounted TV. I stood up, and Antton followed me. Instead of the route map, the TV screen showed blurred images of nighttime Paris. Lights flashing by a tunnel entrance. A smashed-up car. Headlines on loop: Diana, Princess of Wales has died. Diana, Princess of Wales has died. Diana, Princess of Wales has died.

Unable to tear my eyes away, I thought of my mum and Aunty Deb. Diana's death would break their hearts. They had formed their own private fan club, called themselves: LDG, Lady Diana Girls. My mother was a believer and Diana had captured her heart. It was urgent that I call home. The group around the TV expanded, bodies pressed against bodies. People wept, and I placed my hand over my mouth. Diana had been part of my life: her engagement, marriage, and divorce. Fashion, children, eating disorder, lovers, colour of hair. Today, she had died, and everyone kept saying, "How can Diana be dead?" Something had happened, you could feel it in the air, and when I reached out, I could touch the edges of the hole, feel the shape that she had left behind.

I wondered now, if I went back to that journey, if I could have done things differently? Perhaps I should have stayed behind the curtain and not entered the stage? Or should I have tidied Antton up and returned to my duties? Why did the beige not strike me as important as it has struck me now? Did our conversation set into action a chain of events, as some believe the fluttering of a butterfly's wing in Japan can cause an earthquake in San Francisco? If I hadn't met Antton, and hadn't gone near his beige trench coat, could I have prevented Diana dying, and consequently your death?

I wrote in the notebooks:

The mystery of death is unutterable and obscure. When you peel away the surface there is more and then more...

The questions flood my mind: why did I fall in love? Because I fell from the first time Antton said *"Ça va?"* Love tumbled into my lap, and I do not recall Antton mentioning bees, but perhaps there are things I have forgotten. Recently, I dreamt there were bees under the skin of my legs. It was itchy. They were trying to get out, and the bees have entered these pages. Buzzing, they swarm inside, looking for queens, seeking out the best flowers. They collect nectar and pollen, forage to make honey for the cold winter months. The bees work hard, and I put nouns, adjectives, and verbs together to give you honey, my *buba.*

You are a child and I spoon it onto your toast. I spread the honey to the edges. You are an adult and I pass you the jar, and you talk to me about your plans to travel to South America, you mention agriculture and climate change. You are full of future plans. Then I am old, *buba*. You put honey in my chamomile tea, stir it, and put the cup between my trembling hands. You cannot stay for long but will be back soon, and I must keep my strength up.

Buba, in the middle of the Channel, did the bees fly from Antton's mouth, glide round our bodies in the sea, sprinkling nectar and love?

Did their labour distribute sweetness and light?

Before the ferry disembarked, Antton and I exchanged names and telephone numbers (landlines not mobiles) and postal addresses.

"I'll write." He pecked me on one cheek, and then on the other.

Taken aback, I blushed. *"Bon voyage!"* and waved at him as he left, my arm stretched ridiculously high, as if I was a beacon of hope.

Miguel, another steward of my age—who I had never spoken to, and I had been told was half-Spanish and looked like a model—pulled my arm down and whispered in my ear, "You can stop waving now, but what a sexy man."

Unexpectedly I giggled, "Yes, he is." But before we could continue, our supervisor came over, smiling with what looked like intense pleasure,

"The toilets need cleaning. Anna, it's your shift today. Make sure you take bleach, a bucket, and rubber gloves. It's like hell warmed up in there."

"Ladies and gentlemen," a man's voice boomed over the ship's Tannoy system, "welcome to France. *Bienvenue*."

3. We Are All Creatures of the Stars

Energy ran through my veins. At midnight, a male nurse knocked quietly on my door and in a whisper asked how I was doing on my first night. Hiding the sunglasses and notebook, I replied I was fine, and pretended I had just woken, for I didn't want to cause alarm. Hours passed, and I could not stop writing. The sun began to rise over the hospital grounds. The tree branches became visible against the dusky pink, and *buba,* I began telling you the story of the goddess Aurora, who carries the dawn, scattering the sky with roses. Petals occupied my mind, and everything seemed better, the way it is when you receive a small piece of good news after months of despair.

When I finished, my arms ached, and I unclenched my fingers from my pen. They felt stiff, and I went to look at the sky. Outside, a mist hung in soft, low clouds around the trees. Sunlight crept into the grounds. The morning felt fresh and gentle, and I flipped through my night's work satisfied. Tears in my eyes. A sudden sob in my throat.

I had written the word beige.

BEIGE. BEIGE.

BEIGE. BEIGE.

BEIGE. BEIGE...

I had filled twenty pages of the orange notebooks. Some of the writing overlapped, and some letters were big and others small. When I counted them, I had written "beige" seventeen hundred and twenty-five times. On the last page, my pen nib had torn through the paper. The colour had been named.

My *buba,* La Place was built from beige limestone. It appears important to mention this, though the château was more sandy than pale brown. The day we visited, an estate agent, in a creased shiny suit, reeking of cigarettes and aftershave, led us up a steep sign-less track.

"It's a beautiful C15th construction, in local stone. It was a holiday house for a Parisian journalist. He is selling it cheap. Needs money for a divorce," he winked. "It has seven bedrooms and gardens. Very quiet. There is just the farm below."

The property had parquet floors, lofty ceiling roses, crumbling walls, tumbling outbuildings, and we discovered it needed "work." It was what the French call *"un trou d'argent,"* a hole for money. But La Place was lost between valleys in a hinterland, a scattering of *bocage,* a crisscross of fields. Balls of mistletoe hung in tree branches, suspended like giant spheres. Fields of burnt yellow sunflowers turned opened heads toward the blazing sun.

“It is the house I have always dreamed of. Finally, I can make a home outside of the city.” For years, Antton had longed to return to the southwest where he had grown up with his mother. Yet La Place was far from the sea, from the city, from Edgware, from everything I had ever known. Would I enjoy living so many miles from the waves, the shingle, from that great expanse?

“It is nothing like London,” I joked, but I wondered if I would get lost among melon farmers and honking geese, distant from a city’s beat, from the grime, from crowds, exhibitions, and bookshops where I swam like a fish. But *buba,* you must understand, to choose is to renounce. The valley was cut in the shape of my heart.

After our visit, we stopped to picnic at a nearby lake. “Five minutes’ drive, a perfect place for a dip,” the estate agent had explained, the house had no pool, but a nearby swimming spot, an old quarry filled with water. On the sandy beach, Antton made me a *tartine,* spread fresh white goat’s cheese on baguette and added thinly sliced tomatoes, sprinkled with sea salt. As I ate, he stroked my stomach and I bit into the bread, leaving a circle. Everything curved.

“Careful! Pregnancy is a hormonal rollercoaster of emotions,” Rachel warned me on the phone, “I am worried about you planning to live in the middle of nowhere. A woman will produce more oestrogen during one pregnancy than throughout her entire life.” Rachel lectured me on progesterone, relaxin, and HPL. But her jargon sailed over my head.

Buba, I was feeling growth. Instead of being skinny, for the first time in my life I was plump, felt heady and voluptuous. And I experienced a sense of aliveness; something to do with potential; the days radiated. You grew and I grew, and it was like a time-lapse film of a flower blooming but this was happening to me. Life flowed and I was positive that armed with my love nothing could stop me, or us.

“I am round like the moon,” I joked with Antton, on the beach, as we imagined our life in La Place. We were finally together, for much had happened between us. But *buba,* we will get to that later. We were having a baby, and the three of us would live in a lost castle. Antton had his dream job in a nearby *lycée.* I’d had a successful interview with a Monsieur Kassar for his language school. There’d been a rose on his desk, poetry books on his shelves. “Everything is perfect,” I whispered to Antton, and I see now, I was courting disaster, tempting fate. That day, alone on the beach, we stripped naked and ran from the sun into the deepest water.

Hospital meals were served punctually at 7:00 a.m., 12:00 p.m., and 7:00 p.m. in the refectory. Breakfast was chunks of baguette or *biscottes* with butter and jam. For lunch and dinner there was a starter, main course, cheese, and then a dessert. At 4:00 p.m. there was coffee or tea with biscuits. Slowly, my appetite returned.

In the afternoon, people did crosswords and Sudoku in the refectory. A woman often sat, immobile on a chair. I overheard another patient whispering, “She was locked in a bedroom by her parents for eight years.” One day, a naked young man careered, screaming into the room. The nurses caught him, and he was restrained and put into seclusion. Horror drifted past me like a cloud, just out of reach. I avoided Yann, despite his attempts to say hello, but accepted to talk to the Queen of France woman. Believing I was an English aristocrat, she called me Princess Camille and offered me sweets from her pockets, saying, “Us royalty must stick together,” or, “They are preparing the guillotine for us later today. The sugar will sweeten the blow.” Once, she even stroked my short hair tenderly, “You must let it grow back. Princess Camille, your face is beautiful.”

All the staff carried large bunches of keys. Ward doors were kept locked, and we had to ask for permission to go outside. It may seem strange, but I enjoyed being locked in. The terrible anxiety I had felt at La Place waned. Dr. Vidonne came to see me, and I told her I felt safe, but didn't tell her it felt like you were finally safe too. She asked if I had flashbacks and said things could get stuck. But I shook my head, and we booked an appointment for the following week.

Nighttime, I stayed up late and wrote in the notebook. It was fortunate I had a single room because no one could complain. A nurse told me, "There are only seven on the ward." Lists came at night: *1) Yes. 2) No. 3) Maybe—Everything comes back.* Nighttime became writing time. When the nurses' evening rounds were over, I took my notebook and began. Beige obsessed me. I was convinced that there was a reason I had written it down. *Buba*, it was as though I was shipwrecked in the sea and clung to each piece of stray debris that floated past, trying to find meaning in my muddled mind.

I wrote: *Beige could be the reason things got bad.* Beige, it seemed to me, my *buba*, was what we came to expect. It was absence, neutrality, the stifled conformity Cyril sought when he painted our hallways "mole." It was the fallback option, chosen to avoid debate, avoid emotions, avoid life. Yet the placid placebo had an underbelly.

I began to question whether beige was a slow painful departure. I began to question the role of beige in everything. Beige ran through my nights like a creature escaped from the zoo, but I couldn't identify its origins. In French there is an expression: "*Mourir à petit feu*," to die gradually, and this seemed to sum up what beige meant for our world. I wrote in the notebooks:

The expression "Mourir à petit feu" arrived with the invention of the gas stove and the culinary technique of simmering. Beige is like this; it sheds hope like leaves until one day there are none left on the tree. It is the cancer of the soul. A simmered death.

As the light faded, I tried to find the language to reach you, *buba,* something to edge the ever-spreading flood of my grief. A drop of ink had fallen onto my dampened sheet of paper. It spread and spread and would not stop. Each night, I attempted to build barriers to enclose this water. My letters, I imagined, could form dry earth. Mountains could rise from my grieving seas. Between water and earth, we could walk hand in hand. It would be a place I could return to, to go down to the edge. In the darkness I wrote:

What language can contain a dead child and a mother? How can a dead child and a mother speak? Why are there names for someone who loses a spouse, or a parent, but no name for a parent who has lost a child? All that exists is beige babble.

When your father left the ferry, I wondered if I'd ever see him again. It felt like a dream: our night discussion, the awful news of Diana. An hour later, the ferryboat travelled back to Britain. On the return journey, I worked the hot-food counter with Miguel,

"So awful about Lady Di." He was reheating baked beans. Tears came into his eyes. "She was my fashion icon, and so much more." We began discussing our favourite outfits, when our supervisor barked,

"Get on with your work!"

We served all-day breakfasts, burgers and chips, while in my mind I replayed meeting Antton, each word and gesture. And with each recollection, my feelings amplified.

"It's the first time I've seen you smile," Miguel said during our break and offered me half of his Kit Kat, confiding, "I have fallen for an Italian man. He's much older than me and it's breaking my heart."

It was the beginning of our friendship. That summer, I was suddenly no longer alone, or just with Rachel. I branched out and made new connections, for I had always been and would always be a loner. *Buba,* there have been few friendships in my life. Miguel has always been there.

Sociability and bees:

Sociality is variable among bees. Species can be solitary or social. Most species are solitary. Solitary bees do not live in colonies, produce honey, or have a queen. Most bees live alone. We don't imagine this. Humans have always exploited bee imagery as a metaphor for human groupings. Bees were used as a symbol by the communists to explain the natural origins of organized social groups. By Napoleon to represent society and work. Shakespeare used apian metaphors for politics and government.

In strictly solitary species, each female builds a nest by herself. She prepares the nest for her larvae and then dies without ever having contact with either her offspring or other bees, except of course for mating. These mother bees live and die alone.

"Congratulations! I love you!" At a port cafe I finished a call with my mum from a public phone. The day before, Miguel and I had got our A-level results. I had two B's and a C and had my place at Warwick University. Miguel had an E in maths and Economics, but a B in History of Art. He still hadn't rung his family. "My dad is going to kill me!"

As we waited to be served breakfast, I noticed the café owner had stuck pictures of Diana all over his hut. Under the photos, someone had written: "A TRAGEDY" "OUR PRINCESS IS DEAD," "LADY DI! WE WILL NOT FORGET YOU!" and "THE DAY THE WORLD CRIED!"

On the ferries, people talked about Diana constantly. She had died but was still not buried, and a deathly limbo hung over that week. My time was filled in equal measure with contentment, for I was (finally) settling into my job, and the impression that my current hostess's duties included collecting tears, consoling weeping women, men, and children.

"It's outrageous!" The port café owner was berating the Royal Family who hadn't put the flag at half-mast. He handed Miguel his polystyrene cup of sugared tea.

"I'm so hungover," Miguel moaned. The night before we'd been to the pub to celebrate (and commiserate) our results. Nervous, I'd stopped after one G and T, but Miguel had carried on until closing time. Over multiple bags of crisps, I learnt he was wealthy and privately educated (unlike me), but his tyrannical dad—who owned multi-storey car parks all over London—had got him this ferry job "so I would learn the value of work." Miguel laughed and called himself "a gay-boy" and "a sausage jockey," and told me I was "a Jew girl," saying things you'd never get away with now.

At the end of the evening, he started crying and drunkenly clambered onto the seawall. He swayed as inky waves swelled and water crashed against stone. Almost losing his balance, he shouted, "I'm going to jump. I can't go home. I won't survive." He lurched forward, almost fell, and I dragged him down, fighting with him as he tried to climb back up on the wall.

"You can't do that. Miguel, get down! GET DOWN!" Finally, when he stopped wrestling with me, Miguel was sick. We sat on the cold pavement for a while. Neither of us spoke. Then Miguel said,

"I must escape before my bastard dad forces me to work for his car-park business, get married, and have kids." He said he would run away and paint. "Rome is calling me, the statues, the terracotta, and my Italian lover! Look," he pointed to the sky, to the port, "If I painted this now, the shore would tell me something, I would absorb the colour. The stars." We both gazed up, and he grabbed my hand. "Painting is the absolute thing." Then, Miguel stripped off his shirt and raised his arms to the sky and the moon, proclaiming, "Anna Nelson, you are very clever and highly irritating, but you have beautiful hair, and you are my new best friend in the world. I will love you forever as much as I love my Italian lover's dick." He shouted out, "We are all creatures of the stars," and then he was sick again.

Buba, Miguel knew you from when you were born. Delicately, he held your baby head. Bought you the silver mug we kept on the kitchen shelf in La Place. Gave you sketchbooks and crayons. He gave you all of the colours, except for beige. He tickled your toes and bought you shiny leather Italian lace-ups that you wanted to wear to bed. You called Miguel "Uncle Behind Behind Tomorrow," as I tried to explain that I had known him for a very long time.

"Oh, he is Behind Behind Tomorrow," you said, as you hadn't learnt the word or idea of yesterday. *Buba*, how we apprehend time changes with age, and the past, future and present come to mean different things.

Uncle Behind Behind Tomorrow is a painter now. Our friendship is anchored in past time shared. He's living in Rome, makes colours do things on canvas. And knows about the chromatic wheel. He tells me the colours diametrically opposed evoke each other, yellow demands purple; orange, blue. The eye demands completeness. Last time he came to stay, he painted with you, and you told him, "Imagination makes art, it appears on the paper. A splat."

Buba, Miguel is my good friend, he is in my heart, even if he texted me recently:

Anna, I love you and I know you are sad but babe you're going too far.

At the port, Miguel frowned at the egg yolk on my eighteen-year-old chin. Ignoring him, I read the postcard I had just received from Antton. He'd written, in stumbling English:

Dear Anna,

Good to be meeting you on the boat. A meeting of chance, and even if we are all just an infinite chance. We are responsible for this chance.

Today, I am travelling to the mountains, back to my homeland, the Pays Basque. Please write, if you wish. In friendship, Antton.

This formal missive, which I came to learn was typical of Antton, was written on the back of an old photograph. A young woman, in a long skirt and shawl, stood by a large half-timbered Basque house, with a water crock on her head. In the background, a mountain river flowed. Printed at the bottom was a quote about the secret, mysterious, and profound bond between Basque family members. Everything in the picture was sepia.

Even that first postcard was tinted with beige. Beige is different to brown. Brown is the colour of the earth. Unless cremated, we'll all finish in the ground, positioned as in sleep. Eyes closed. Dreaming. Horizontal. Few cultures bury their dead vertically.

The day after your cremation, *buba*, we put your ashes in the cemetery ground. I wanted to climb down into the grave, lie by the urn, beside you so you would not be alone. I regretted we had not left you whole, because I could have held your hand. By the grave, I turned to your papa, and we held each other. The grave's earth was not insipid or pale. This is what confuses me. The earthen brown was different to treacherous beige. The brown of the earth felt like something true. It was, I wrote in the notebook: *unthinkably real.*

At the port I held Antton's postcard, grinning, Poets write that love elongates time, and in that moment the scene before me expanded, the squawking gulls, the ringing sound as halyards hit metal masts. Wind blew sails into motion. A French man had sent me a postcard. Lonely Anna. Skinny Anna. My heart blossomed. I couldn't believe he'd got in touch so fast. Miguel snapped,

"Who's the card from, fat-arse?"

"None of your fucking business. Don't be so rude!"

Miguel grabbed Antton's postcard and then, having read the message, he chucked it back at me and walked away without a word.

That evening, as the boat left port, we sneaked out onto the deck and watched the land shrink and disappear. He reached for my hand on the railing, I almost pulled it away, still smarting from his rudeness, but he said:

"Anna. I am sorry about earlier." Holding onto the rail, we stared out at over the stern.

"It's so strange that we use the same word 'wake,' for the white line left by a ship in the water as for the party after a death." Miguel looked at the waves. "I don't know what I am going to do. But, if I could paint, even paint something like this night... If I could paint these white lines or orange lines, it would change everything."

Under the emerging stars, I forgave his sharp tongue, as I have learnt to do throughout our friendship.

"I am just jealous. I haven't heard from my Italian lover. That French guy is cute. GFI."

We cracked up laughing. GFI, go for it, was a phrase that Miguel's cousin, who worked for the family car-park business, used to motivate his team. Go. For. It. Aim for the best. Get out of bed. Put on the tie. Make the call. Do not put off for tomorrow what you can do today. Looking out over the darkening sea, we squeezed our hands tight. Was GFI possible for love or canvases? Miguel needed to close his eyes, leap through the dark and paint. Yet nothing was certain, we both knew, even then:

love was wild. Love was lucidity and blindness. Love brought you together and could tear you apart.

"Good morning Camille." In the refectory, Yann carried a breakfast tray. He smiled politely. "I am sorry for disturbing you in your room. But, when you are feeling better, I will show you around the grounds. Please," he pointed to a chair. I sat down, exhausted from my sleepless nights, wondering if my first impressions of him had been wrong.

"I hope your first couple of weeks have been alright?" We tucked into coffee, baguette, butter, and apricot jam, "But I wanted to give you some advice. Just avoid the Friday fish but take seconds of the Saturday couscous. And beware of that patient"—he nodded toward to a short old lady, in a purple dress and slippers—"who is a kleptomaniac and thinks she is Marilyn Monroe, and this one." He glanced over at a young obese man, eating his way through a tower of *biscottes*. "He can be dangerous, stabbed another patient and does the most terrible farts." Yann winked but didn't mention the Queen of France woman so I presumed she must be safe.

I yawned; all that mattered was my notebooks. The first one was full and I was halfway through the second. My body ached from tiredness, but I needed to get through the day, so I could reach the night.

"Hello," the dark-haired nurse sat at our table and glanced at her watch. She smelt of stale cigarettes.

"How are you, Madame?" Not wanting to talk, I looked away. "Are you OK?" she repeated. Ignoring her, I put my cup down too hard and it landed with a sudden bang. She stared, and insisted, "Are you OK?" and I found myself shouting,

"FINE. FINE. FINE."

I regretted my cries, for everyone in the refectory fell silent, and I could feel the nurse's eyes run over my badly cut hair, sloppy clothes, and my sunglasses. It felt like she could see inside me, to my failure.

For, *Buba*, I was a mother who had lost a child. A careless act. I *was* responsible, for how many mothers lose their children. I guessed the dark-haired nurse had read my medical file. The nurses knew you had gone, and she must have learnt about the accident, in French *"ta disparition."* The word seemed appropriate; you had disappeared. The surface of the world, like a sheet of water, had closed, smoothing over what they called your death. But I knew you were alive somewhere.

I had to find you. But first I had to work out why you had gone, find the explanation in the notebooks. There had been a lack of concentration, a lack of devotion, a lack of being a good mother. The dark-haired nurse must have noticed this lack. *LACK*, I wrote on the whiteboard at the language school, is a deficiency, a shortage, a want. I had suffered from LACK, perhaps a lack of observing beige. I was beginning to understand. The price had been high. I had lost my son and I needed to find the bees. They were whispering in their swarm.

"Do you want some more baguette?" Yann passed me the breadbasket, and I looked over, grateful for his conversation. In the refectory, everyone began talking again, getting ready for the morning group activities, a workshop they called "gymnastics for the brain." When I tried to go back to my room, the dark-haired nurse informed me I was strongly advised to attend the therapy group. There was no choice.

Later, we did puzzles and verbal reasoning games called Hurray for Change and Writing in the Stars, and I noticed Yann's brain worked fast. Amongst us all, he always had the first response. At the end of the session, he announced he'd prepared questions for a special nautical-themed quiz and, *buba*, this is when I began to think of him as a boatman.

He asked:

1. If an ocean current is a continuous, directed movement of seawater, what are the different forces that change its direction?
2. What is the busiest shipping route on the planet?
3. What are the origins of the name "abyssal plain," the area of the deep sea, at the very bottom of the ocean?

A patient complained, "Yann, only you know the answers to your questions."

He responded, "I'm Breton, born to be on water. I've sailed all over the world, spent months without seeing the shore. The sea is naked. That nakedness is never the same, like a lover that takes you a different way each time, but always beautifully."

No one spoke for a while. One nurse chuckled, and the dark-haired nurse frowned. The Queen of France woman murmured next to me: "Winds, water density, and tides all influence currents, along with the earth and the sex life of the nobility. Up and down, and up and down." Chuckling to herself, she walked out of the room as I raised my hand. "I know the answers to your second and third questions."

Yann smiled, and I felt the water rise between us. There was a liquid bridge. It was like the birth of the English Channel—or *la Manche* if you are looking from the French side. Fifty million years ago, it was a shallow valley, a riverine network. The rivers connected Britain and Europe. A mega flood overflowed, and an island and continent emerged. The sea, I realised, connected Yann and me.

My *buba*, water is the liquid ingredient in this story. As any cardiologist will tell you, 73 percent of the human heart is water.

From the back of the room, I gave my answers. "The busiest shipping route on the planet is the English Channel." Yann nodded. "And the abyssal plains are the deep sea at the very bottom of the ocean." I sighed. "I think the word comes from the

Latin "unfathomable," and these plains cover around half of the planet." Closing my eyes briefly, I imagined the plains, ripples and whispers, a perpetual unexplored darkness.

An experiment regarding bees and darkness:

A recent experiment shows the majority of bees immediately plummet to the ground when the light inside a room is switched off. They lie on the floor waiting for illumination. What scientists find surprising is that it's such a sudden switch-off. Like the bees are hard-wired for dark=no flying. Nothing moves in the shadows for these bees. Nothing happens at night.

When I met my future mother-in-law, she showed me her beehives. When I was nineteen, Antton and I drove over the Pyrenees, from Donostia into green valleys that seemed to have no end. He explained his mother had brought him up in France, but then she returned to her Basque village to retire, because the Basque have a special relationship to their land. "We have a saying that when we're far from our home, we are lost."

In the car, we passed through isolated villages where the graffiti was of a raised fist. In hushed tones, Antton told me, "It's like the English and the Irish. The Basque want independence from Spain."

When we arrived at Katixa's house, it was raining, a light drizzle. We got out of the car and Antton said, "The Basque call this particular type of rain *xirimiri*, pronounced shiri-miri. When I feel this rain on my face I know that I am home."

Later, we watched through the kitchen window as two old women dressed in black walked through the garden. Antton explained his family's house was close to the church: "Funeral processions and church-goers walk through our garden. The mourners have a right-of-way. A path of mourning they call a way of the body. The path to carry the dead."

As he spoke, I pictured a long thread connecting Antton with his past. It stretched through his body, his mother, into their garden, into the dead, to the valleys, the mountains, and the bees. I pictured our Edgware house, the beige walls, and the Meccano wheel. There was emptiness between me and my ancestors. "The blank space on my family tree is enormous," I said but Antton didn't seem to hear and put his coat on, saying, "I need to go and see a friend."

Your father was a specialist at leaving me, *buba*. He'd walk out the door for five minutes and get back in an hour, arrange to call me in the evening, and then go to meet a friend. It was as though he constantly needed to walk away. It still makes me furious.

In the village, Antton left me with his mother. It was awkward, as we'd never met. We returned to the wooden hives, built on the ground her family had occupied for centuries. It was still raining, and she said, "Rain always brings good luck. If you die on a rainy day it is a sign your soul has been saved." After, we watched a TV show in Basque (which of course I didn't understand) and we made dinner. Her knife sliced through red peppers, and I asked about a bowl on a shelf, and she explained that when she was a teenager, she helped her aunt prepare for funerals. Washed and dressed the deceased. "We women would stay up all night, watching over the body. Mirrors were covered so the soul would not fly away. We put salt in bowl, like that one, for the dead." She chopped through an onion and told me that at funerals she dressed in a black mourning cape, accompanying the coffin. Carrying a candle, bringing the light. Katixa bore light made from Basque bees' wax, the nectar of flowers.

But my mother-in-law died long before you were born, *buba*. The house was passed onto a cousin and the hives destroyed. If she was here, Katixa would have told her bees of your passing.

At night, she would have watched over you, offered a bowl of salt. At your funeral she would have found a woman to walk behind your coffin, with a basket filled with bread. A female neighbour would have carried rolls of beeswax (*ezkoa*). This neighbour would be the bearer of light. Katixa could have called the wild bees as well. She could have summoned all the Basque bees, and the bees of Europe. She could have brought them, in swarms, flying onto her land. There would have been a cloud, a darkened, buzzing sky made of millions of bees.

Should Antton have found a way to tell the bees? A relative, neighbour, or a friend needed to tell the swarm. In some Basque villages, it was said that if a stranger mentioned a death to a hive, the bees would attack them. Had the bee on the door handle been carrying a message from the other side? My little Lou, have you been lacking light? Did no one give you salt, or a candle to guide your way? Are you wandering the abyssal plain, in perpetual darkness? Did you get lost on your way?

A fortnight later, I saw Dr. Vidonne in her consulting room. Even now I remember her quietness, and if I could draw her voice, it would be a straight pencil line, sketched by hand, imperfectly regular. Her quietness didn't signify disinterest. She was attentive to my every word, and inside her room even my most terrible thoughts were welcome.

"How are you?" she asked, and followed with a series of questions, leaving me time to answer each one.

In those early days, I barely spoke, mumbling, "I don't know," and "Fine. A little better." She nodded and took notes. Then, she told me I was to be moved to the open ward. "You seem a little better, Madame. It is time to move on."

Surprisingly, I found I was apprehensive. I felt safe in the closed ward and had even stopped fearing myself. But she said, "You will be fine."

The staff returned my belongings, my phone and all my clothes, and luckily, on the open ward, I got another single room. The rules were less strict than in the closed ward, and with no obligation to leave my bedroom for evening meals, I now worked on the notebooks more and more. Antton had dropped off spare clothes and I had asked him for more notebooks, specifying they had to be orange.

I wrote:

I don't want to sleep. When I wake up, sometimes I remember things, but I cannot write about them. They come when I wake up and so I don't want to fall asleep. It makes my insomnia worse. Dr. Vidonne asked again about flashbacks. She says this could be part of what led me here, to my breakdown. She said normal memories transform throughout lives, but traumatic memory never changes. Traumatic memories remain exactly the same. Trauma returns in flashbacks.

But I haven't told her. I can't. It would be opening Pandora's box.

In my final weeks on the ferry, Antton occupied my thoughts, and the wind whipped at my hopes. At 4:00 a.m., preparing for early morning departures, I put on standard makeup, an itchy uniform, tan tights, and pulled my hair into a bun. Miguel pinned my hat to my head. I followed regulations and toed the line. Outside, the sea was navy-black. Orange street lamps glowed. Tarmac glistened, tickets were checked, and polite conversation was made, and I pictured Antton, his smile against the blue. A longing for my mountain man lifted me.

My supervisor informed me, "Your work is improving." The disorder of water and love knocked me into shape.

When I glanced out of the portholes and saw the waves, I thought of Antton, and I could cope with the complaints from the middle-aged men about the pale colour of their toast, drunk teenagers, and wailing babies. Miguel and I giggled as he pointed out the French rural boys dressed in New York street clothes, and the chic French women in green quilted Barbour jackets, sipping herbal tea with milk, which they thought was "so British." We kept our distance from the rough Jersey girls drinking port and brandy at 7:00 a.m. because they were on "a fucking holiday."

We sailed between Britain and France, between Portsmouth and Cherbourg, between Saint-Malo and Poole. It was a steep-deep blue coming and going across a narrow arm of the Atlantic Ocean separating the southern coast of England from the northern coast of France. I watched the red journey tracker and tried to find Hurd's Deep, the spot where I had met Antton. Could I relocate this precise place in the sea?

One of the crew told me, "It's exactly like on land, there are coordinates and a travel log. Captains write down where they are, where they're going, where they've been. The spot you describe is a mile deep. Such a lot of water!" He said the complete replacement of the water in the Channel took days and months, "new water comes in and old water flows out," and I thought about how everything begins again and again, can be reused and rethought.

On the ferry, when the land had disappeared and there was just sea around us, every dream I had felt achievable. Was I running away from reality? Was my new life an escape? As I think of this, *buba*, it seems important to remember that in water things are felt in a different way. For example, sound waves travel five times faster in water than in air. My friend Rachel has explained this to me, saying, "Water sound waves don't vibrate in the inner ear. They go straight to the skull."

Dreams on water take a different form, daydreams and those of nights.

I recall one night: tucked into my sleeping bag, Miguel describing his domineering father throwing away all his soft toys when he was ten, telling him, "You have to grow up!" Then the plans he was making with his Italian lover: "He wants me to live in Rome."

"You should go," I said, for as I heard the wind blow around the ship, it felt like we should be free as the gusts of air. No one should stop us going where we wanted to be, we should paint, travel, and read. Our dreams should guide us like the wind. For the crew said: the wind is strong, warm, clean, cold, briny, brisk, brash, clammy, keen, fresh, cold, salty, contrary, bitter, cool, soft, strong, bleak, stiff, continual, warm, dank, crisp, joyous, sweet, open, sharp, low, wet, clean, honest, usual.

As I laid my head down, I longed for Antton beside me. Rocked by the waves, I dreamed of fish, swimming pools, and corridors. They say love is blind, but *buba*, wherever you are, know this: love is lucidity. In love, contradictions become cohesion. The net becomes lace. The knots keep the sails high.

But I ask myself now, was I longing for Antton or for the ocean? Little Lou, the word "longing" exists in English but cannot be found in French. Travelling constantly on the sea is like living in translation. After a while, I never knew whether I was coming or going. The vibrations and rhythms of belonging yanked me back and forth.

3a. Things Have to Be Broken for There to Be Change

"Good morning!" Yann was at the foot of my bed. "You missed breakfast." He smiled nervously and, clasping his hands, he leaned down, "Change is coming, Camille. I need to talk to you. We must go on a journey in my boat Little One Hold Tight. We must leave together. As soon as possible. Go to the sea!" Pacing my room, he launched into a speech, "Did you know that Camille backwards is Ellimac, and a random rearrangement of the letters in your name will give Amlciel? Did you know there have been many, many famous Camilles: women and men, painter Camille Pissaro, tennis player Camille Pin? Sculptress Camille Claudel understood about change. She was an artist. They said she was Rodin's muse, but what if it was the other way round, what if Rodin was her sidekick? What if things were the other way round?" Yann proclaimed his sentences like a chant. "Camille burnt all her sculptures when she sought transformation. When bad things happened, she took a hammer and smashed. Things must be broken for there to be change."

"Please, Yann. Give me a minute. Let me get dressed," I tried to interrupt him, for Yann was frightening me. He walked around my room picking things up and putting them down, practically jogging from place to place.

"I haven't slept for two nights. They say I am going into a manic phase. But obviously they," he spoke so fast I could barely understand, "merely want to stop me in my flight, for I have understood about change, but also a thing about my childhood, about how to get things to change. I must get back to Brittany, I must get to my boat."

It was then that I noticed that he had grabbed one of my orange notebooks, had curled it into a tube and was clenching it tight.

"Put that down!" I got out of the bed. He handed me the notebook.

"I'm sorry. I'm sorry, Camille," he repeated quickly, "very sorry. Really sorry. You see, my mother beat me with a ladle when I was young." He began laughing. "I have never told you this before. We lived on an island, Ouessant, off the Breton coast. My father was never there. He was a fisherman in the New World, catching cod. We were alone with my mother for months on end. I was her scapegoat." He grimaced, exposing his gums, "My mother beat me so hard around the head that I have constant tinnitus. A bell never stops clanging in my ears. When I worked as a sailor, I used to love storms, as the sound drowned out the ringing. For the first time in my life, I could hear something else." He paused and I noticed Yann was lacking a few teeth. "They say my mother was like a stone without a crack, she had no love in her and would not be opened. You have a crack running through you, petite Camille, but it is where people can come and meet you, they can get inside, and that is why we are friends, need to get my boat and go out on the sea. Did you know?" Yann began shouting. "DID YOU KNOW CAMILLE THAT IN QUANTUM PHYSICS THERE IS A THEORY THAT TIME IS LIKE A BALL OF WOOL? IT WRAPS AROUND AND AROUND ITSELF TURNING IN A CIRCLE LIKE A SKEIN OF YARN AND TWO DIFFERENT BITS OF TIME CAN TOUCH EACH OTHER. THAT MEANS THAT THE PRESENT CAN TOUCH THE FUTURE OR THE PAST. THAT MEANS THAT YOUR SON..."

"What is all this shouting?" A male nurse burst into the room, and Yann began running. The nurse chased him, saying, "Get out of this room. You need to calm down."

Yann raised his finger to the sky. "I have a boat, called *Petit, Tiens Bon.* Little One Hold Tight." Then, he whispered in my ear, "Camille, if you want. We could find the things you're looking for. We can take my car and drive to Brittany. We can cross the sea." He nodded toward the orange notebooks and left, slamming the door. The male nurse sighed, "Please ring your bell if he does that again."

Getting out of bed, I put all the notebooks together, wishing Yann would return. I wanted to know more about the boat and his time theory, the ball of wool, and I wondered what he knew about Louis. I didn't recall mentioning that I had a son.

I wrote in my notebook:

Buba, if time is like yarn, and we can jump between different bits, then I can see you.

The following night on the ward, everything was quiet. It was my favourite time of day, around eleven, when it felt like the night was a stage, the curtains could rise and I didn't know who would enter or what would happen. As I looked over my notebook pages, there was a knock on the door. It was late. The knock came again. I hoped it was Yann.

Instead, a young nurse came in, her face lit by the corridor's glow. She seemed hesitant and smiled nervously. "*Bonsoir, Madame.*" There was something flower-like about her, or at least that is what I remember, she was like one of those pale moonflowers that bloom at night. The nurse was willowy, with short, highlighted hair, and a fringe skimmed over her eyes. Something about her reminded me of someone else.

"Can I tidy your notebooks?" she said.

I nodded. By now, I had already filled several notebooks.

Some had tumbled onto the floor. It wasn't just writing, I had also been gluing things onto the pages, and tracing over and over the words. The writing soothed me: *BEIGE*. I would write: *BEIGE, BEIGE, BEIGE*. The nurse placed everything into a pile. On top, she put the small picture of a boat that Yann had given me as a quiz prize.

"Oh, that's a great photo. I love sailing," she sighed. "I went sailing for the first time a couple of years ago. It was life-changing. It struck me that on a boat we're completely free. We have everything we need to go anywhere in the world. Bunks, a cabin, a kitchen—"

She stopped and put her hand in front of her mouth, and I wondered if she thought she was being too personal. Again, I had the sense of déjà vu. Quickly, she pointed, "I see you haven't taken your pills," and she handed me my medication, a glass of water, and watched as I swallowed. We didn't speak for a while, and I liked that she stayed silent. She walked back toward the door, and then turned, red-faced, "Sorry, I forgot to introduce myself. I am a new nurse; my name is Agnes."

As she spoke, it hit me, the young nurse looked just like Lady Diana. I wanted to leap out of my bed and stand close to her. By the open door, she radiated, as though she carried something inside and whatever that was, it was made of light. Then she said "good night" and was gone.

My heart fluttered. I was trembling. The nurse Agnes was a sign. All my life flags had arrived on my horizon. Reality was presenting the path ahead. Diana had returned. She had been there the day I met Antton in the middle of the Channel. This was perhaps the gift I had ignored for so long: the gift was knowing where to look.

Quickly, I removed a pill from beneath my tongue, wrapped it in a tissue and stuck it under my mattress. Since I had been in the hospital, I took all my medication, except the sleeping tablets. The nights were long. I had much to do.

In the following hours, I wrote in the notebook:

Diana has always been part of my life. "She was not a conformist," Aunty Deb said, showing me the photo of Diana holding the hand of a man with AIDS. The surrealist artist Leonora Carrington was a Diana fan! Diana was a goddess. A free spirit. The People's Princess. PP. Check the letters. P is the 16th letter of the alphabet. 1+6=7. Seven the magic number. The seven wonders of the world. The neuropsychologist told us today, "The longest sequence a normal person can recall without help contains about seven items." Check this. Seven.

Diana was named after the protector of animals. She had force. The Greek goddess Diana was a hunter.

I added later, scrawled in the margins: *statues of the goddess Diana from the Anatolian city of Epheus portray her covered in eggs, identified as BEE eggs. A QUEEN BEE lays tens of thousands of eggs in her short lifetime.*

What is the link between Diana and bees? Lou, you were never seven.

On her honeymoon with Charles, they made Diana wear beige. A beige tweed, a beige jacket and skirt. It swung round her thin legs. Rough fabric. Highland setting. Castle. Green grass. His hand is on her shoulder. A heavy royal hand. The beige crushes her delicate frame. Old beige caught Diana. Beige is a net of tradition. Smothered by the family beige. Beige seeped into her skin. Beige for the princess. Beige for the prince. Did they make her wear beige to bed or virginal white?

Trapped by beige. The first computers were beige. Sand coloured. Tan. To wear beige on a honeymoon is to know marriage is work. Days are work. Nights are work. You must make love or fuck beige, even awkwardly. Be beige to earn your keep.

My mum said, "Diana is anorexic." Only ate nothing, probably only ate beige food. Beige food does not provide nutrients. Eating beige is like eating photocopy paper, envelopes, and tape. Eating work. They say that people who like beige prefer fading into the background rather than being the star of the show. Beige people are supposed to lead quiet, clean, dependable lives. Lovers of beige, it is claimed, get on with everyone and could only be criticised for being afraid to take risks. All of this is LIES.

When I had finished writing, I lay back, satisfied. It was 3:00 a.m. The night is blind, I thought. But my notebooks were a canvas and here the night's blindness revealed something else. Antton had always needed eight hours' shut-eye and got frustrated when I didn't sleep. "Night is my fertile ground, my gathering time," I explained. The night hesitated, tripped, moved backwards, woke up with a start. Doubting everything, the night questioned relentlessly. Hypotheses emerged as rough sketches and vague premonitions. The night altered the way I thought.

In the hospital, my nights became a workshop for the impossible, for *buba*, at night I could get close to you, and you emerged logically. In the night, I didn't want to read, but to write you into being. In my white room, we could play games, and I pictured myself cooking your tea and brushing your hair. I threw a ball into your arms and caught it when it was returned. You told me about your fears. "Heights are frightening," you said. "I am scared when I am up high, and the ground far away." At night you whispered to me, "Mama, I am on the other side," and I descended the steps, went to Hades, and found you. I did not "move on" as there was nowhere to go. *Buba* at night, I rocked you awake.

I wrote:

Throughout history, bees have been used in many cultures as a symbol of immortality. Bees do not stop.

A couple of days later, I bumped into Yann at lunchtime. Each of us carried a plate of yellow paella rice dotted with red peppers, green peas, and prawns. Yann was yawning and had bags beneath his eyes.

We sat down together. I had dozens of questions to ask. But when I said "Hello" he ignored me and ate, mouthful after mouthful. A few grains of paella rice stuck on his chin, but he didn't brush them off. "Yann," I said, "I want to talk about your boat. I want to drive to Brittany, and then cross the sea. I need to talk to you about my son."

His shoulders slumped, and he didn't answer, stood up, and began walking away. He stamped his feet on the floor. "Yann, please," I said. "Explain about the ball of wool."

But Yann had gone, and that afternoon I overheard two male patients saying he'd got into a fight with the dark-haired nurse, smashed a chair, and been restrained. Currently, they said, he was in seclusion in the closed ward. "He's always going up and down, and up and down. He bounces back here like a ball every few months."

That night I couldn't sleep, and the night after. Finally, I gave in and took a sleeping pill. I wrote:

They have begun invading my mornings. Every day. I cannot stop them. Cannot tell Dr. Vidonne. She asks again about flashbacks; she asks quietly and when I don't answer she smiles. But I don't know what to say; how can a colour be a flashback? And why are there smells and sensations?

Beige is pretending that there is no invisible life.

Late September, I finished my summer job. Carrying my rucksack on my back, I returned to Edgware, to our house, my childhood bedroom, and my books. Red-eyed, my mum opened the front door, yanked me to her chest and squeezed me tight,

"I missed you and I miss her terribly." She was talking about Diana and me. We hugged by the Ferris wheel.

"I am still grieving," she told me the next morning, "but we might get a timeshare in Marbella." She flicked through catalogues and blew her nose.

"Don't count your chickens before they're hatched," Cyril said, using the hodgepodge of cheap wisdom he shoved into every conversation: "Before you look round it will be Christmas." "It's all swings and roundabouts." "Actions speak louder than words." "It's all part of life's rich tapestry."

Buba, I think now, as I am older and possibly kinder, that Cyril used these sayings as litanies or spells. He repeated clichés and adages every day as though they were pegs, and could attach the kite of his life to the ground. Sometimes I wonder whether Cyril lived in fear and if proverbs gave him the courage to brave the flight.

That September, he adjusted his glasses and added figures to a handwritten document entitled: *Hypothetical Simulation for Possible Purchase of Timeshare.*

"You're so good with figures," my mum glowed.

"Have I told you that joke?" He turned to me. "How many accountants does it take to change a light bulb?"

Raising my eyebrows, I stayed silent.

"Two. One to change it and one to make sure it was done within budget." He burst into high-pitched giggles. My mum laughed, but I wasn't sure whether she was faking it.

Yawning, I ignored them both, leaned against a counter, and flipped through the *Jewish Chronicle,* reading announcements of deaths, births, bar mitzvahs, and bat mitzvahs. Holocaust stories. Photos of Lady Di's funeral. My mother pointed to the pictures. "It wasn't an official state funeral. But in the streets outside Westminster Abbey, there were two million mourners, and I was there. The coffin seemed so small. I went to pay my last respects with your Aunty Deb. It's the best thing I ever did."

Lou, here are five details from Diana's funeral and death that have been acknowledged in the press (except for the last one):

1. Despite being only fifteen and twelve, Harry and William were allegedly instructed not to cry at their mother's funeral.
2. Diana's brother gave a controversial eulogy, speaking of how Diana was "sneered at by the media" and "talked endlessly of getting away from England."
3. Harry and William didn't want to walk behind the coffin.
4. Initially, Diana's funeral wasn't going to be public.
5. The colour beige can be clearly identified in documents surrounding her death. When Diana's sister flew to Paris with Prince Charles to bring Diana home, photos of her leaving the hospital show she is wearing a beige coat. Diana's sister is walking next to Prince Charles. Jacque Chirac, the French President, is just behind her. Diana's sister's dress is black, but her coat and scarf are beige.

Upstairs in my bedroom, I was cursing Cyril and his Ferris wheel when I saw the time on my radio alarm clock and shouted, "Fuck!" I was going to be late to meet Miguel up in town, in Trafalgar Square.

"I'll take you to Gabies for falafel sandwiches," he'd said. "Then we can go to the Portrait Gallery." Miguel sang down the phone, "The Only Way is Up."

My *buba,* eighteen is a special age. When I was eighteen, in Trafalgar Square, Miguel and I ran past the tourists and the pigeons, we ran toward our futures, toward paint and open seas. We ran toward everything.

Buba, you will never be eighteen. I have nostalgia for this. I miss the days, years, and futures you will never live. It is odd to miss something which has not happened yet.

You will not... I write on the paperboard at the Centre Via Langues. Monsieur Kassar looks in through the classroom door. His face expresses sadness as I explain:

"We use WILL to speak about the future. It is always combined with another verb. In the negative, we add NOT to the end of WILL and not to the main verb. (= will not)"

Examples:

> Your boy's limbs will not get seal-slick wet or turn brown this summer. (correct)
>
> In autumn you will see not leaves turn red, watch them fall like orange rain. (incorrect)

Buba, your future will not unfold. Winters will not come, or the spring. You won't ask me, "Why does a tree grow up into the sky, instead of down?" Or "Where does the white go when the snow melts?" Your mind will not leave early childhood and turn to maths, adding and subtracting. Your shoelaces will be left untied. Your teenage years will not arrive. Your first kiss. A sprout of hair. Anxiety. You will not ignore me as I pick up your dirty socks, shouting, "You treat this place like a hotel." We cannot argue, furiously. You won't slam your bedroom door. We will never read newspapers with Antton over breakfast, discuss French politics, or list our five favourite films. We can't ride rollercoasters, eat hot dogs, watch trash TV, go to classical concerts in Budapest and after—in the darkness—catch winter snowflakes on our tongues. You will not learn the fear of death.

You will not travel alone on a ferry, train, or plane. You will not leave a wake behind you. Or fall in love. You will not feel the rush of eighteen.

When I was eighteen, *buba*, summer pushed the doors wide open. The world was a pop-up book. Possibilities rose from each turning page.

My bags were packed. I had a grant to live on and a room in the Halls of Residence. Tuition fees were free. I was the first person in my family to go to university. My mum kept clutching my arm, "We're so proud," and she took pictures of me to send to Aunty Deb. For three years I was away. Three years later, my graduation picture adorned her living-room wall. *Buba*, do you remember when you saw the photograph, you thought I was a pirate in a tricorn hat?

"She graduated in French, I think. Took an option in art and philosophy, but I don't understand it." My mum laughed nervously, and I laughed nervously too. But I wondered if she hadn't had to leave school at fourteen, learn shorthand, and become a secretary, if she would have studied French, philosophy, and all the rest. Philosophy, I hear that word in her mouth. It meant one thing to her and another to me. Our signifiers and signified did not match. For her my degree was a symbol of success. It's like that joke about the Jewish mother, standing on the beach, calling out to a stranger for assistance, "My son, the lawyer, he's drowning."

Yet, my degree identified me as something else: I now belonged to a different class, another part of society. "I'm practical, I can't do all that thinking," she would say, bowing her head over a recipe book or a fashion magazine. Miguel lived with her briefly during those three years I was at university. After trying to work in the family car-park business, he was kicked out of home and had nowhere to go. She made him packed lunches when he worked in hotels, went to night school to do a fine art A-level and applied for art school. “She’s like a mother to me,” he would say, while I grimaced.

“I am a mum first and foremost,” she would assert to new and old friends, met in waiting rooms, on buses, in queues, and at neighbouring restaurant tables. Since you’ve gone, *buba*, my mum rings and texts every day: *How are you? I love you. LOVE. Love you,* she writes. There is an L, an O, a V, and an E, and I look at these letters. They are in front of me and I climb them, like ladders, slip and fall. My mum puts the ladders back up, every day.

Buba, I worry that I was not this kind of mother. You did not always come first. When you cried as a baby, to finish a book I ignored your tears. You watched too much TV, while I prepared classes. Whenever possible, I jumped on a train or plane, so I could get to the sea and be alone. I ran away, and toward Miguel in Spain, Italy (or wherever he was living), or to Rachel in London. I loved you, *buba*, but I needed to be free, and Antton scared me. Too ready to settle down. At La Place, he planted trees in the garden, saying, “I will see them reach maturity.” Perhaps he was a good dad, and I got it wrong.

Talking about my responsibility is like wrenching oysters from a rock. It requires a sharp blade and the deepest cut.

When I admitted to Dr. Vidonne, “Of course the accident was my fault,” she told me, “There are things in life we can’t control.” She said I must forgive myself, yet forgiveness for a mother with a dead child is pointless, for I accuse and then forgive myself each hour of each day.

But the *why* of your death haunts me. How it could have been avoided, and I wonder: could we tell the story of a life through all the deaths we escaped? Could any existence be plotted by the moments we brushed up against the Angel of Death? Can history be written about absence, what didn’t happen, like walking through the looking glass?

Is that where you are, *buba*? If I break all the mirrors in the house, will I find you on the other side? Should we have put shrouds over the mirrors like the Basque and Jews to stop your soul escaping? If I go into your bedroom and tap on the surface, will you open the door and let me in? Should I smash the mirror and set you free? Do we all bump daily into the Grim Reaper, or the Canaanite god of death connected to a Phoenician god who they said was made of mud, and was also the source of life? Do we teeter haphazardly between birth and the grave, waiting to trip? Is it true that luck is just a destiny we ignore, a destiny written with invisible ink?

Here are examples of when I should have died, but:

1. The time I got the flu, age three: "You had a temperature of 104 degrees," my mum said. "We had to take you to the hospital. They said it was very serious." I should have died, but...
2. On the M25 London motorway, my mum remembers, "We drove into the pile-up, and our car went under a lorry and the roof of the car was pulled off but we were safe inside." We should have been killed but...
3. My cancelled New York weekend with Miguel in September 2001. We had tickets for a MOMA exhibition *I Am Still Alive.* But Miguel tripped in his studio and broke his ankle. We cancelled, and the Twin Towers fell. "It was meant to be," I told him. We should have experienced death but...
4. All the instances when your papa wore the beige trench coat. We must return to this, *buba*, for it keeps crawling in. Each time he wore the coat we were walking on a tightrope, the tightrope Antton often mentions. He says "Life is like walking on the thin thread of a spider's web, stretched over an abyss." Everyone can fall...

Why do we rise or fall when we die? Is it just a question of gravity? Like the stairs at La Place, there are things left at the bottom, and things left at the top. In these orange notebooks, I write from top to bottom, from left to right. I write in the hospital, and later I wrote on Yann's boat. Purcell plays in my head on repeat. "Dido's Lament," sung by Jeff Buckley. Jeff can enter my repertoire, as he is deceased. Only grievers and ghosts can come inside. Jeff died by accident, swimming in a river, and I want to ask him whether the beige coat floated beside him. Did bees fly near his body as he drowned? I have no evidence. No facts confirm this, but Yann told me the mystic Breton people believe that when someone dies, the soul is released from the mouth as a bee. An insect emerges from the mouth of the dead. It flies onwards.

Jeff sings "Remember me. Remember me" in a high-pitched tessitura, the story of Dido, whose lover is tricked into deserting her, resulting in Dido's suicide. Dido asks to be remembered but to forget her fate. But how can I forget your fate, Lou? It is an outrage, an inconceivable thing to ask a grieving mother to forget their child's fate.

4. The World is Always Ending Somewhere

"I still sail whenever I can," Agnes said. A cold fog lingered, and yellow pockets of daffodils emerged from the gloom. The nurse and I walked briskly through the hospital grounds. We wore hats and scarves and tucked our hands into our pockets. It was March and I had been in the hospital for nearly a month. It was six months since *you* had gone.

"Where do you sail, Agnes?"

"We spend a lifetime running after our lives!" Yann interrupted us. Red-faced and panting, he had jogged up the footpath. He jumped back and forth and rubbed his hands together to try and keep warm.

"Hello Yann," said Agnes, ignoring his strange outburst. Things like this often went unchecked by the staff—digressions about secret gods, sudden cries, revelations about death threats transmitted through TV screens. There was an acceptance of what could be considered rudeness, oddness, or madness. A calm silence was one of the answers.

"We were talking about sailing." I hoped Yann would join in the conversation. He had returned from the closed ward and seemed to be better. I'd been waiting to hear more about his boat, Little One Hold Tight, and his plans for our journey.

"I'll always remember my first time sailing," Agnes continued. "Until then, I'd lived in the mountains. Grew up with a climbing harness round my waist. A friend invited me for a weekend sailing. There's a weird feeling the first time out, the boat tilts as it moves. I kept asking myself: will I fall, will I fall?"

Yann frowned. "But the keel under the boat weighs almost a ton. It prevents it from tipping. Falling is very unlikely."

"Yes. But I remember my first time," I said. "One of the ferry crew took me out on his yacht, and I tripped over the boom, threw the wrong rope, got confused by the sails and the constant preoccupation with the wind. I rarely went again."

We stopped at the top of the steep path. From here we could just make out the hospital buildings, cloaked in fog. I stamped my feet to try and keep warm. Yann looked at us sternly. "On a boat the elements are always in control. The water and the wind take over. On a boat, to move forward, you learn to adapt to the wind and the tides, and not the other way around." He stared at his hands and seemed lost in his thoughts.

"The principle of reality is important to apply to all life situations! It's the difference between what you want and what you're able to do." Agnes glanced at her watch. "Oh! I must go, I have a meeting. Don't forget you both have a therapy group at eleven."

As she walked away, I went to speak to Yann, but he ignored me and turned to follow Agnes.

"Yann?" I called out, "I want to talk about your boat and sailing in the Channel. I need to go."

Yann stopped but didn't turn around, "I can't talk now, Camille. Don't forget you're grieving. Don't forget I am ill. We've got to focus on getting better. I want to get back to work. They have offered me a new job in the forest. Work will do me good, and you must say 'Goodbye.'" He spoke loudly as he walked away, as though he was trying to persuade himself. "One must adapt to the wind and not the other way around. It is essential."

I found myself alone, bewildered, in the fog, my plan to talk about our journey thwarted. Why had Yann said I should say goodbye? I thought of you, Lou, and I saw us together on that path, on that cold morning, and I reached down to hold your hand. In my mind, you wore mittens, and I whispered to you,

"Hello, *buba.* The fog will lift. Don't be scared, *buba,* I am coming."

My bones and muscles folded, as a bird folds its wings. I wanted to tell Yann nothing had changed. I wasn't interested in getting better because I wasn't ill; there was no need to say goodbye. I just needed to follow my heart. There was a connection between my heart and you, *buba.* My heart's chambers opened and closed, and I remembered Miguel showing me a C13th text on hearts, describing the *fiery force (that is, the vital spirit).*

My fiery force was driving me toward Yann's boat and you. My heart burnt all obstacles: the idea of getting better and grief. I was not grieving, I thought as I walked back along the foggy path, Yann had not understood. There was no need to grieve, I loved you with all my heart and I knew I would bring you back.

A few days later, I bumped into Yann in the refectory. It was lunchtime and they were serving *cassoulet,* the South-West stew of slow-cooked sausages and beans.

"Come and sit." Yann looked surprisingly cheerful. "I have good news for you!"

Around us patients and staff joked, there was a cheerful mood. Everyone enjoyed it when *cassoulet* was served; it was the same with couscous, or choucroute. These dishes were special treats.

"So, what's the good news?" I dipped baguette into white beans and tomato sauce.

"I changed my mind about sailing. The wind has blown me toward you, Camille, and I must adapt to the elements." Yann stared at me, and a mist came over his clear eyes, and they turned a milky blue, then changed again. "Change is calling. Oh, change always calls me, Camille. It will be a dangerous journey, but I must get back to Brittany, to Finistère. I need to get home, there is a pearl in an oyster. We can sail out over Biscay, through Plymouth."

At the sound of these sea areas, I remembered listening to the radio shipping forecast, on the ferries. A crackling voice predicted the weather of our days, "Plymouth, Biscay, Trafalgar, FitzRoy, Sole, Lundy, Fastnet, Irish Sea, Shannon, Rockall... Gale warnings in force. General synopsis. Area forecasts: wind direction/speed. Weather. Visibility." Even now, when my insomnia was bad, repeating the sea areas was like a lullaby.

Yann talked louder. "I need to get home. We can take my car, drive to Brittany and get the boat. She's still in storage at the harbour, and doing fine. But there is something I need to know." He looked at me. "Camille, I worked as a skipper. I can't set sail without coordinates. Where is it you want to go?"

My hands began to tremble. I couldn't speak. I thought that Yann knew our destination.

"I can't explain." I stood up, bumping into the side of the table, my sleeve caught the handle of my fork and I tipped my plate. The white beans and sausages fell to the floor. Everyone stared. The dark-haired nurse arrived by my side with kitchen roll, a mop and bucket. "You'll need to clean that up, Madame," she said. But I couldn't do anything. Instead, I ran out of the refectory and, back in my room, I wrote in the notebooks:

BEIGE. BEIGE. BEIGE. BEIGE. BEIGE. BEIGE. BEIGE. BEIGE. BEIGE. I filled page after page, until I was calmer.

Buba, perhaps I should explain how I got to the psychiatric hospital, before I describe when I left. Perhaps I should tell you, after you'd gone, what led me inside where madness lurks? Before you died, I had taught euphemisms to foreign medical students studying mental health. A crossword puzzle was provided with clues to revise the colloquial vocabulary:

Nervous. Troubled. Bonkers. Off your trolley. Crazy. Insane. Non compos mentis. Barking. Lunatic. Yet I use the word "mad" deliberately. For, *buba,* even if we've tried to banish asylums and straightjackets and airbrushed pop stars and celebrities talk of depressionconfusionbipolaritydisturbancetraumapeopleonthes-pectrumaddictionserotoninthebrainflippingthelidanxietyobses-sivebehaviouraldisordersorgeneticillness, we still fall back on a common word to describe our tap dance on the edge of chaos. This word is "mad."

Inside the hospital, even the Queen of France woman adopted this everyday lingo. The day I dropped my plate, she came and murmured in my ear, "You are not mad, Princess Camille. Just filled to the brim with sadness."

Yet, before my hospitalisation, I remember one or two days when I was "mad." Perhaps I have blanked out the rest, and I wonder if they are like the flashbacks, events that Antton refers to, and I cannot recall. Dr. Vidonne told me, "Sometimes it is better to forget. Your brain is shielding you from danger." She added, "The world is always ending somewhere."

I thought, somewhere there is always someone falling apart. My madness was a disconnection that felt both leaden and airy, heavy and light, and I suffered from wave after wave of fear. One thinks of madness as a split-second transformation, but my experience was gradual. A sensation of falling. The gods doodled a zigzag on a piece of paper. My line went down, up, and down again.

It was bad that first winter after you'd gone. Time weighed down on me, I was exhausted. The dishwasher stopped working, both our cars broke down. The house was cold and dirty. The bills left unpaid. We were both on sick leave. In late December, after an uncelebrated Christmas Day, Antton tried to chop down the fig tree in the garden, and I found him on his knees weeping in the mud: "I can't do it." I said it was only a tree, even if I knew it was not just a tree. But he replied he couldn't bear seeing the tree. He booked an appointment with our GP who prescribed sleeping tablets and recommended he see a psychologist. He followed the advice, and the fig tree stayed in the garden, and Antton went back to work.

"I can barely teach," he said when he returned from the *lycée* exhausted, "but it helps me to think about something else."

But I stayed on sick leave. That winter, I didn't want something else, everything needed to stay the same. I was anxious, and night after night, I barely slept, checking locks and doors. I was convinced someone was trying to break in, and for the first time in my life, I was terrified. In the end, I contacted a security firm, and Antton was furious when he discovered I'd spent thousands of euros getting cameras and a security system installed.

"You've emptied the bank account. What about the roof?"

But I had to protect you. Water could drip through ceiling roses and down the walls because my job was to maintain sameness: the sunflowers, the fig tree, and your bedroom. Nothing could change that might stop your return. You were inside me, *buba*. You were in me, and I had to keep you safe.

In the hospital, when I described this to Dr. Vidonne, she said, "These are symptoms of hyperarousal." Taking an article from her desk, she read out loud, "Hyperarousal is a severe symptom of PTSD, a disorder which can dramatically change your life. A fight-or-flight response is perpetually turned on, a state of permanent tension. This can lead to a constant sense of suspicion and panic."

I remember one particular day in January when things took a different turn. First, it seemed better. Late morning at La Place, my telephone rang. Monsieur Kassar left a message in formal

French. "Madame Nelson, Anna. I am ringing, with the utmost care, to see how my dear teacher is and if you plan to return. You are missed." Hearing his voice, I pictured his paunch, suit and tie, pink pastel shirts. The rose on his desk. The pile of poems.

His voice pulled me from my bed: I had to get up, get back to work, perhaps read poetry. We needed money. I took a shower, brushed my hair, stripping knots from my curls. After days in the same pyjamas, clean clothes felt odd on my skin. Rachel had called the night before. "You must eat," she said. As the kettle boiled, I cut baguette, went to get milk. But each gesture felt strange, like I was making breakfast for the first time. Outside the kitchen window, the sun shone. Down the hill, at Devant-La-Place, the chickens clucked in the yard. I thought of you, *buba*. You often climbed onto the kitchen stool, demanding, "I want to see the chickens!" and I almost stopped when I pictured you.

In the notebooks:

Two thousand years ago, Seneca wrote a consolation to a grieving mother: remember, life is a vase that shatters from the smallest shake. The flowers tumble. The water flows. Fortuna is a fickle thing.

In the kitchen, I looked at the clock, back out of the window. The chickens were in the yard. *Buba*, you had gone. It turned like a merry-go-round: you and the chickens, the chickens and you. I poured milk into a mug, added a teabag, but the merry-go-round turned again. Rachel had said, "We often make strange decisions when difficult things happen. The adrenaline lowers logic. Intuitive behaviour takes over. The reptilian brain, freeze, fight or flight." The merry-go-round whirled. The kettle boiled. I poured hot water into a cup decorated with flowers. Roses. Monsieur Kassar's flowers from the Bekaa Valley. At the table, I sat, the hot cup between my hands. There was a pile of Antton's marked essays. The corners aligned. His red correcting pen on top. It was soothing, some things were still the same.

But my hands trembled as I sipped the tea, and I spilled a drop. It splashed on the table. Why wasn't I on the kitchen floor instead of sitting here? Where were you? *Buba! Lou!* I glanced at the essay on the top of the pile, and read the title, first silently, and then out loud: *What is the Meaning of Laughter?*

I pictured the chickens at Devant-La-Place and you on the stool. I began to laugh. It was horrible, but I could not stop. I remembered your favourite joke. The only joke you told because you were six, and had only just learnt jokes. "Why did the chicken cross the road?" "To get to the other side." It made you laugh, the idea of the other side. "Where is the other side, Mama?" You pointed at the door, at the big mirror on the wall. "Other side!" you yelled. Then, you jumped across the room, out of my arm's reach, as I tried to catch you, shouting, "I am on the other side."

In the kitchen, I giggled, chortled. I couldn't stop. It was like laughter in an exam hall, at a formal dinner. Laughter in a synagogue, a temple, a church. Laughter in a silent room. At a funeral. It burst out of me.

In the essay, the student had written that laughter emerges at the tipping point between intuition and reason, between what should happen and what should not. I opened my mouth. My body bent double. I was shaking. I was the mother of a dead child. On the other side. A dead mother.

The laughter stopped the merry-go-round. Instead, it felt like I was turning, giddy, floating, weightless, and when I stood up to catch my breath, I stumbled and sent my cup and the tea flying onto the essays. Clumsily, I tried to gather them together but the tea spread, from one paper to the next. Instead of letting them dry, as Antton told me afterwards I should have done, I took a paper towel and tried to mop up the stains. The sentence *"laughter allows elasticity"* ran into *"something mechanical encrusted on the living," "body"* dribbled over *"mouth," "life"* smeared over *"death."* The more I tried to clean, the worse it got.

The essays were all wet now, and I laid them over the kitchen table. They were unreadable. Closing my eyes, I laid my face down on the papers. Ink marked my cheek. I thought about you, and sitting up, I took Antton's red correcting pen. It was then that I really fell. Yet I felt light, weightless, as though I'd let go of everything.

Over the students' philosophical essays, on top of their smudged sentences, I wrote:

What if Orpheus managed to bring Eurydice home, I wrote, *what if he got her from the world of the dead and brought her back to the living. Can I bring buba back?*

When Antton came home, he lost his temper. Then, he sat at the kitchen table and wept. But my eyes were dry, and I went to bed. The following morning, he left early. In the bathroom, I noticed I had snagged a nail. I took scissors from my bag, planning to cut the nail but instead, when I looked in the mirror, I reached for my corkscrew curls. That is when I fell again. Carefully, I cut off a lock. But once I started, I could not stop. Impatiently, I hacked until mounds of black fluff piled up on the floor. When I looked in the mirror again, I was unrecognisable, like my former self had gone.

"But it is better this way!" I tried explaining to Antton that evening.

"Why did you do that?" he kept on asking. "Why are you destroying yourself?"

I wanted to tell him there was a thorn inside me, but if I pulled it out I would die, because it was that thorn that was keeping you and me alive. Instead, I said,

"I can't lead a normal life anymore."

"But we have to get back to normal."

Stroking the few tufts of hair left on my head, I then told Antton calmly, "In that case, I will probably die."

That is when he made an appointment with a psychiatrist.

A week later, in a sterile surgery, Dr. Vidonne smiled at me, but not brightly. Antton told her you had gone, and he was worried about me; I had stopped sleeping and barely ate, and was irrational. Recently, he coughed, I had "cut off my hair." Dr. Vidonne asked me how I was, but I didn't answer. Then, she asked whether I had dark ideas—*les idées noires*—a euphemism for suicidal thoughts. Despite wanting to lie, I said "Of course" and bit my lip. She followed up by enquiring if I'd planned something, and I looked down, stroking the back of my head where I was almost bald.

Beyond the farm at Devant-La-Place was the old quarry filled with water. The picnic spot where you'd grown from a curve into a baby. Moving from water into air. The lake where you'd learnt to swim. The bank where it was dangerous to jump in the winter, and reeds tangled around ankles.

I stared straight into the eyes of Dr. Vidonne. She was small and slightly built with curly greying hair. Her calm, even gaze swept over me, steady as a lighthouse illuminating my darkness. I couldn't lie to her. The truth was heavy; gravity pulled me down to earth.

"Of course, I've made a plan," I said.

I remember this:

Buba, when you were five, you told me:

"When I'll be grown up this will be the olden days."

"When I grow up I'll be a man or a fireman or a cat."

"When I grow up I will be a cooker."

"When I grow up I will make books."

Even before you learnt how to read, you spent hours, cross-legged, turning pages. You said, "Mama, make me a house of books," and I took novels, dictionaries, reference books, and volumes of poetry, linguistics, philosophy, and anthologies of short stories, and built three walls; flung blankets over the top to make a roof. Carrying a torch, a plate of sliced apple, and Lala your rabbit, we crawled inside. When Antton got home, he joined us, and the three of us lay "like sardines." We giggled as a book by Saussure fell on Antton's head. "We are fish swimming across the pages," I said. "The perfect mixture: water and philology."

You said, "Next time Uncle Behind Behind Tomorrow comes. We will paint you on a red boat, Mama."

One day, you drew me on a red boat. Miguel gave you wax crayons, and you drew my red body. My red head was round like the moon. My boat's sails were red, and red books cluttered the deck. Above red clouds floated and you sketched red waves, a choppy red sea. The red anchor was hoisted, and red wind filled the sails. I headed toward the red horizon, sailing away in your red boat.

My little *buba*, are you taking notes from this book as I write, are you using a keyboard or a pen? *Buba*, if you are reading these sentences, draw the boat. Add Yann, the boatman. Add your papa, he is calling your name.

An ancient Japanese philosopher believed that somewhere there was a library, containing archives of all the words, in all languages: slang, literary, polished, idiomatic, and technical texts; manuscripts, scrolls, bestsellers, and brochures, pamphlets, and recordings, hardbacks, letters, and lists. Carefully preserved and classified, there are songs, slogans, and film scripts, jokes, and sermons. Diatribes and cartoons, myths and dreams.

When I have finished transcribing my notebooks, I will walk through these library doors and seek out the Department for Miscellaneous: Lost Souls. In an aisle, marked Diverse Orange Documents of Differing Dimensions, I will place my notebooks on a shelf.

I will tell the bees where I have left the orange notebooks; I will whisper it inside the hives. Politely, I'll ask them to give you the message, to fly to you, *buba*, on the other side. Bees' role in connecting flowers and pollination outweighs the importance of their honey chores. A third of crops rely on insect pollination. The bees must be kept alive to connect, pollinate, and deliver words. Survival is about communication and links between things, networks, alliances: pollen, bees, love, and flowers, beige and boys.

My *buba*, are you walking along the library corridors? Have the bees dropped sweet nectar into your ears? On your tongue? Are your hands touching spines, seeking out titles and authors? Have you selected a book? Do your eyes look through each page? Are you reading me, reading these notebooks in the library? Louis, I am trying to show you a way home.

At Warwick University, I shared a room in Halls with a girl with a double-barrelled surname and a swinging black bob who bought all her clothes in pairs. Like many of the students, she had been to private school, and seemed shocked when I took my books out of a box: Sartre, Camus, Leonora Carrington, and Marguerite Duras. "You seem quite educated," she said. My copy of the racy romance *Riders* (Rachel's favourite, particularly the sex scenes) was stuffed at the bottom of a pile. On the wall above my bed, I stuck Antton's postcard.

During Freshers' Week, Rachel came for twenty-four hours, "to make sure you get properly settled in." When I look back, I remember Rachel wore a yellow and black jumper, striped like a bee. Was this a coincidence?

In the hospital, I copied the following text into the notebooks under the title

BASQUE

In the Basque country, the bees make the wax used to make the argizaiolas—wooden tablets wrapped with a wax candle rope. The flat tablets are carved, often in the shape of bodies, decorated with rosettes, crosses, vegetables, and leaves. The argizaiola is lit by the etxekoandrea, the woman of the house, or the eldest daughter, and placed on the tomb. The candles are lit several times a year. They burn for several hours, sometimes a day. They offer the souls of the dead the warmth of home.

In the Halls, Rachel and I were drinking chocolate Horlicks from dirty mugs. My roommate had gone to the pub. "He's almost seven years older than you!" Rachel shrieked. I had just announced I was in love with Antton. She grabbed his postcard off the wall. "You barely know him, and he sends you a picture of women carrying water on their heads. Probably wants you at the kitchen sink."

"Don't be so uptight! You slept with that twenty-year-old guy who was going out with your cousin. Do you remember we called him tetrahedron because he had so many love triangles?"

Rachel pursed her lips, and then giggled. She had an active love life, whereas mine had just begun, and after that summer, I would turn in circles. She pulled a self-help book from her bag: *How-To-Meet-Your-Perfect-Man in 5 Easy Stages.*

"You need to make a plan." She placed her hand on her chest. "I swear I will not get married until I am twenty-six, have graduated from medical school, and become a brain surgeon. Then, I'll find a husband," she flipped through the book, "who is from the same social-economic group as me. Another doctor or a scientist. I will wait until I am twenty-eight to have my first child. I'll have the second at thirty. Then we'll buy a holiday house in France, or in Italy. I will lecture on TV."

"What about chance..." I was mulling over an idea that had just come to me, days on water. The endless sea. It was there, and always there. "I could work on the ferries."

Rachel looked at me, incredulous, and tapped my head, "Don't be stupid. You're far too clever. You can graduate, then do an MA. You could be a teacher."

I snorted, but I was used to Rachel. Her mind stretched out into the future, over the years, flew around the world, from London to New York via Hong Kong, where she was planning to spend a year studying brains. All I thought was that I wanted to go back and forth over the Channel, spend time in libraries, and see Antton again. I didn't tell Rachel I'd fantasised about our Paris wedding. It was an urge, a flight of fancy. I had no idea.

After I received Antton's postcard, I sent one back, with a picture of the Channel. Weeks became months, and we wrote and wrote. We would write to each other for three years, writing more often than we met. Waiting for his letters was such sore unpredictable pleasure, would they arrive this day or that? Simultaneously my student life continued. I spent hours in the library, Miguel visited, and in the Student Union, on Gay Night, we danced to Abba. Encouraged by Miguel, I flirted with a Dutch drama student, got drunk, and lost my virginity. "That's great," Rachel said, when I told her on the phone. "But be careful. You need to make friends," she warned after I also admitted I spent most of my time alone. As I grew up, Rachel always seemed to be telling me something as though without her I would "lose control."

But I felt free, that was all that mattered to me, and I wrote to Antton and later, inside postal sacks, our epistolary exchange mixed with other letters: reclamations, misinformation, and indoctrination. Conversation and hot air. Our missives crossed over the Channel, travelling by air or by boat.

Dover–Calais Dover–Dunkirk Newhaven–Dieppe Plymouth–Roscoff Poole–Cherbourg Poole–Jersey and *Guernsey Poole–Saint Malo Portsmouth–Cherbourg Portsmouth–Jersey and Guernsey Portsmouth–Le Havre Portsmouth–Ouistreham Portsmouth–Saint Malo Rosslare–Cherbourg Rosslare–Roscoff Weymouth–Saint Malo.*

At first, Antton, signed his letters *"Amitié,"* "In friendship," later this became "In great friendship," then *"Je t'embrasse,"* which is difficult to translate and halfway between a kiss and best wishes. He was a nearly twenty-five-year-old French man writing to a British eighteen-year-old. It was *risqué*. He wrote from libraries, from his study, and from the teacher's common room where he complained:

It is boring in this room, except when I am catching the headmistress drinking Cognac stored in her desk drawer and she invites me to join her.

He wrote to me in broken English and French.

What do we mean when we describe someone's language level as "broken"? As though we demolish a language when we are learning. In fact, we are inventing, making something new.

When you were born and when you died, I had to speak in French to the doctors, the neighbours and the mourners. I lived through your life and your death in translation. I hated it, the not knowing what to say, not the right phrase, tone or the precise words. At the funeral home I didn't know the correct vocabulary to describe ashes, or urn, or the cleaning of your small body.

Antton wrote to me, in response to one of my letters,

Language circles around experience, like the first hunters trying to catch a beast. But I don't know which is more powerful or important, what we feel in life, or what we try to say?

Buba, your geography began in a correspondence, letters sent between a small island and France. Your papa and I drew love lines between destinations, sketched a future into which you would be born. Following our writing, we travelled toward each other, through tunnels, over steep bridges, we caught trains, flew in planes, and embarked on ferries. Our tickets were checked, our passports controlled.

Yet, when we crossed borders, none of the officials looked for love. No one scanned for you. We had passports stamped, our bodies searched for hidden objects, weapons, glass, guns, scissors, knives, and things that cut. But no one checked for your destiny. We had no boxes to tick. Nowhere to identify your fate. No one asked:

"Madame, sir, are you in the process of making Louis?"

"Do you recognise that if you continue meeting, a new human being, Louis, may be born?"

"Sir, do you know that this child, Louis, will change your lives?"

"Madame, do you take responsibility for the fact that the course of time will be modified?"

"Sir, have you thought about beige?"

"Madame, do you accept this child will die?"

No machine drew the outline of the trajectory of your life. From those first letters, all these paths led to you. Take a pen, *buba*. Hold it in your hands. The first lesson in geometry: look at the starting points of each line. Euclid described a line as a "breadthless length." *Buba,* everyone makes a shape. Join up the dots. There is a point where the axes meet. You were born here.

"You should have met more often," Rachel berated me later. "Then things wouldn't have got so complicated. You know over 90 percent of communication is non-verbal. Love," she believed, "Love happens in real life."

Buba, she was wrong. Love can happen in letters and in poems. At the end of a long day, Monsieur Kassar tells me, "Poetry is as necessary as breath." Love happened with your papa. In real life and in letters. Our love was there at first sight, at last sight.

Our letters wrote you into being, and after you had gone, the paragraphs and sentences became a cipher. Unpacking old boxes of correspondence, I tried to read your riddle, go back to everything that had led to your being here. For weeks, I wondered if I broke your code, could I bring you back to life?

"You need to leave the past behind," Antton pleaded when I sent him messages about this from the hospital. For a while, I sent him a text each day:

What is death? It is impossible. I am frightened. Where is Lou?

Things keep happening when I wake up. I don't know what I am remembering.

Perhaps, I am falling apart.

It was spring. Outside my hospital window, the birds sang. That morning, Antton had rung. "We've booked a social worker appointment for you, just to set things straight, all the practicalities: our finances, the debt, your job. There is no rush. But when you're ready to come home, we can turn the page. My psychologist told me..." Antton talked about new beginnings, grief and reconnecting, and I held the phone away from my ear. Increasingly, my dealings with Antton were strained.

Buba, I do not want you to think I didn't love your father; but our paths were separating at this point. Antton was working, saw friends, had got a quote "to fix the roof." He was imagining the future. During a recent visit, in the hospital café, he'd said, "Your hair is growing, and you look better," and "when we can," and "when the time is right," but I didn't know if I would ever be right/ready/better. That morning, on the phone, I answered, "Yes, darling," and wrote down the social worker appointment date. Then, I said I had to dash, as I had a session with an occupational therapist to work on my autonomy. It was a lie.

Instead, I went outside where a soft blue sky broke through the clouds. Yann followed me up a path, the edges lined with primroses. It was never easy to walk with him, for he stepped here and there, scampering like a goat. As we walked, he laughed, telling me about how he'd won his car, a yellow 2CV, in a bet with a tree surgeon. He'd dared Yann to move one hundred logs in one hour. "I did it. I did it and I got the 2CV!"

The sun shone and the weather was finally warm, and I was wearing my sunglasses, but lifted them up to feel the heat on my face. Most of the time I still kept my sunglasses on, although the staff often asked me to remove them for group activities. Yann and I walked up to the steep part of the grounds, and then down the other side of the valley. Here the path crossed by an old cemetery, for the hospital had once had its own graveyard. Dandelions, wild grass, and weeds grew between the tombs.

"They haven't buried anyone here for over fifty years!" Yann said.

Resting between two moss-covered graves, I ran my fingers through my hair. It had grown out into a ring of black curls, and I remembered an article I had read that week in a dog-eared copy of a magazine,

"Did you know, Yann, in the middle of the Mediterranean Sea there is a Greek island where archaeologists found an infant cemetery? Thousands of babies were buried there inside amphorae. Their little bodies held in cooking pots."

As the infants were not considered full people, they could not be buried in traditional graveyards. The place was unique, and researchers believed the most realistic theory to explain the existence of this rare cemetery was that there had also been a birth sanctuary on the island. Inscriptions were found mentioning a goddess of childbirth. The place was for midwives and mourners.

Yann listened to me, and for a while he stayed silent, and it was quiet in the cemetery. Then he said, "It was the same in Brittany, on our island Ouessant. My grandmother helped with births and washing and dressing the dead. One day, she took me with her, and I watched her strip a dead man naked, wipe him clean, smooth the tension from his face. She said giving someone 'a beautiful death' was the best gift."

Clouds drifted in the sky, and bees buzzed among the wildflowers.

"Camille, you don't need to explain about the Channel," Yann said. "Just tell me where you want to go, and I'll take you. In Breton legends, there is a man who accompanies the dead on his vessel. I'll be your boatman."

The sun shone in the sky and I felt the heat on my bare skin. A breeze. The trees swayed. Yann took my hand and led me from the cemetery, and we walked back to the hospital without a word. We left the bees and the dead behind us, but I knew we would return.

For university Easter break, I went back to London overnight. The following morning, I was flying to Paris to see Antton. It was late evening when I arrived. My mum was wearing more makeup than usual, smelt strongly of perfume. I had cut my hair into a bob, wore one large earring—stars and moons dangled from my ear. As we hugged, my earring caught in her off-the-shoulder jumper. But before I could shout, she put her finger to her lips, hissing,

"Cyril has colon cancer. He's been ill for three months, but he's reacting well to treatment. Don't say anything."

Shocked, I raised my eyebrows. In the hallway the Ferris wheel turned. The lights had been put on. Cyril had placed tiny flowers around the wheel. In her passenger seat, the old lady with the cat had a daffodil in her basket. When I saw tears in my mum's eyes, I hugged her again. Throughout that evening, I held her tight.

"You are here, at last." Antton met me at Charles de Gaulle airport the following day. I remember he was wearing the beige trench coat, and he put his arms around me, and I was suddenly awkward. It was my first visit, our first weekend together. He barely spoke, so I remained silent, and we caught an overground train, and then a Metro. At Belleville station, we walked down streets with Chinese restaurants, a Mosque, cafés, Arab and Jewish corner shops. The area reminded me of Edgware. "Edith Piaf was born here." Antton tried to make conversation. On a terrace, a group of old women played cards, roared with laughter, and drank lemon tea.

"I can't wait to get out of here. I want to move back to the Pyrenees," Antton said. Nodding, I wondered what it meant to return to a mountain.

"Do you want a glass of Muscat?" he said later. We were perched on the edge of his sofa bed. From a wall cupboard, he took a red bowl and filled it with black olives. Everything was tidy, bare. He poured us two small glasses of sweet white wine. His telephone rang, but he didn't pick up. The air was solid in my throat. Rachel had warned me to be careful, and had given me a rape alarm "just in case."

On Antton's shelves were hundreds of books. There were names I didn't know and titles I could not read. In the Parisian flat, I didn't know what to say, and I was worrying about my mum, and thinking Cyril might be very ill. But I imagined Miguel saying, "*Oh la la*" and it made me feel much better. Then Antton took my hand and said,

"Anna, may I kiss you? You are a very troubling woman."

I use the word troubling here, but the translation is wrong. He meant, *Anna you make me tremble, you confuse me, and you trouble my water.* I nodded, and he kissed me.

From that moment, I knew I had not been mistaken. At the beginning love is silent cinema, *buba*, I think it is better to think of it that way, like a black and white film, a plot involving skin, smell, and touch. Antton stroked the back of my head. He kissed me and I tasted olives on his tongue. When I looked into his eyes, I was no longer bothered. He gave me such a desire to love. I leaned in and kissed him again. Over the weekend, we devoured fresh croissants for breakfast, walked in the park, ate Chinese noodles and *steak frites.* Over a Tunisian couscous, Antton told me about his past relationships. I nodded and tried to look like I understood. In a bar at the end of the rue de Belleville, we drank "twist," beers with lemony syrup, and Antton said,

"If you look right out of the window, at the horizon, you can see the Eiffel Tower lights twinkling."

The last day, we went to a Rothko exhibition. Back at Charles de Gaulle, we walked hand in hand. In the airport crowds, I wanted to shout out, "Look at us. We are in LOVE!" In the airplane, Antton's kisses were on my skin, feverish and free.

Back in London, it was Passover, and my mum—to my great surprise—had decided to do a traditional meal. Normally we never celebrated Jewish festivals. She and I laid a white, embroidered tablecloth that I had never seen before. There were wine glasses by the plates, even if no one drank, fresh flowers, and an extra leaf in the table to accommodate Cyril's family. Aunty Deb couldn't come, and I hadn't seen her for months. Apparently, she'd sent me a letter from Torremolinos.

"His chemo is working!" my mum whispered. "Just don't mention anything. He's so brave." I wanted to ask how she was doing, but guests arrived, and our seventy-year-old neighbour Betty shouted in my ear,

"Did you know your Aunt Deb has moved in with that Spanish woman? The widow who had the hair-dressing salon."

My mum walked back into the kitchen, our conversation over. Betty yelled again, "You're back from university. Clever girl. *Mazeltov. Nous pouvons parler en français*?"

"*Oui*," I answered, and we started talking about Paris. Before long, Betty was asking about Antton, "my handsome Frenchman," and without thinking I had taken photos out of my bag. Antton and I had taken them during my visit and had got them developed at the airport before I left, "for a souvenir." Within seconds, I was surrounded by a crowd of hands, reaching in for the pictures, commenting on Antton, asking loud questions about his age, profession, wage, favourite colour, family, siblings, parents, divorced or dead? Even if I had been brought up in a sort of Jewish home, the months away had changed me. At university, I'd got used to Christian English silences, questions left unanswered.

"Shall we start dinner?" I asked, trying to change the subject, but nobody was listening. Cyril held out a picture of Antton,

"Nice coat your friend has. Very smart." In the photograph, Antton was wearing the beige trench coat. It was taken in front of the Musée d'Art Moderne. We had waited for an hour to get into the Rothko exhibition and seen large abstract canvases in orange and red.

A guide told us, "Rothko believes if you stand in front of this painting, you become the colour, entirely saturated."

In the picture, Antton's trench coat blew in the wind. My face was flushed, as we had just kissed, or at least, that is how I remember it. When I kissed your papa, I believed it would never end. *Buba,* love needs eternity to exist. Without eternity love is nothing. Everything was framed in that photograph: my smile. Antton's smile. Our held hands. Moons and stars dangled from my ear. The art museum wall and a poster of the orange Rothko painting. The sun casts shadows on our faces. The beige trench coat.

"Where did he get that coat?" Cyril asked.

Buba, you never met Cyril. I only knew him for a few years. He was ill for eighteen months. He never saw me graduate. Never went on the cruises he and my mum planned. Didn't get the timeshare or the retirement gift from his accountancy firm. Never was properly old. After my spring visit, his cancer spread. Did Cyril see the beige coat and in consequence did his cancer cells multiply? Until then, he had reacted well to treatment. From the day I showed him the photo, everything went downhill.

"It's all swings and roundabouts," my stepfather said to me on the phone, quivering, as he got sicker. In the hallway, the Ferris wheel turned, but the carriages got dusty and no one removed the dried flowers. During my second year of university, he died. The wheel was taken away. I never knew what happened to it.

"It is what it is," a friend of my mum's commented at his *shiva,* trying to cheer things up. During the three-day open house, organised by his religious family with death prayers, tea, and cake—four hundred people came to our home. They flooded into the hall, kitchen, and living room: his colleagues, friends, relations, and people from the synagogue. When I opened the door, they looked me up and down. I barely knew any of them. Hands held teacups, mouths munched on sponge cake, pastries, and mini bagels. It was suffocating, like a huge unwelcome hug. An endless chain of hands and arms linked through time.

I wonder now whether I should have gone back to Edgware when you died, should I have buried you among the Jews and pushed your coffin, in a bare wooden box? Should I have let people come and hold your soul as it left your body, for was the *shiva* not a party to light the way? Should I have found my father, and got him to sing Christian hymns? Later, I learnt that if an infant died before being baptized, the Basque buried the children in the roofs of their houses. Did they want to keep them close or let them fly?

After Cyril died, when the cups had been washed and the cake crumbs hoovered, my mum swiftly emptied out his clothes. Acceptance and not-making-a-fuss hung over our house, necessary like a swipe of bleach. She rarely spoke about him, and by the time I was in my third year of university, it was the two of us again. It was as though Cyril had been a glitch. Except our house was still beige, the colour he had chosen for the walls. It was like all the colours had bled from our home, leaving the mole hallway and the straw shade of the settee where my mum sat alone eating bananas every night. She took extra Xanax and began having a social life. Surprising myself, I missed the Ferris wheel.

Years later, my mum gave Antton her recipe for Passover biscuits:

½ lb of either ground walnuts, hazelnuts, powdered almonds, or desiccated coconut, 2 egg whites, 4 ounces caster sugar

(If you like whole almonds or hazelnuts for decoration, you can use them like studded jewels.)

She taught him how to make them, said, "You cannot make or eat just one of these little biscuits. Their size and taste means you need to eat two, four, or five at a time. Bake six dozen. Bake for the world." Passover biscuits had to be served alongside a feast of cakes.

Afterwards, Antton made the Passover biscuits. Lou, you helped him mix the beaten egg white with ground nuts and sugar. He wet his fingers and rolled the mixture into tiny balls, dotted them with whole nuts. You placed them on baking trays, and he put them in the oven. You made tens, dozens of these biscuits. A gathering of planets in the cosmos.

Buba, when I think back to the Paris photo, I feel sure the beige trench coat was an emblem, a sign, a symbol of death like the circle crossed through with a diagonal line, a belt tied round a waist. The beige was a Grim Reaper, an hourglass, or a bomb, timing our left lives. The trench coat was cursed from the day that Antton bought it. And several times, I have asked him about that day. From the hospital, I texted Antton questions, but he told me I was not making sense and that he had picked up the coat in a shop. Yet, in the Paris photo there is a shadow, something out of sight, creeping into those first kisses, planted inside our new love. Perhaps I should have whispered: "*kenahora.*"

My mum always said this word. As soon as one of us mentioned something good, she interrupted me, Cyril, interrupted herself. "You're a clever girl. *Kenahora.*" I hear her say it as I write this. She said it when you were born, "*Kenahora.* He is so handsome. *Kenahora.*" In Yiddish, *kenahora* means, "May you not be cursed." It protects against the evil eye.

My mum's voice is gravelly. Set curls wobble by her chin. Too many cheap, gold-plated rings are shoved on her pudgy fingers. Rolls of fat jiggle beneath cheap, freshly ironed clothes. They are laundered with cut-price detergent. She is smart, likes small treats, and finds bargains. Coupons. Offers. Two for the price of one, and a bottle of pop free with five portions of chips. Finish your plate. Eat up. Smile. *Kenahora.* Take a photo for the albums that only date back to your grandparents because before that everyone is dead. You look well. *Kenahora.* Don't lose your looks, money, or life. Don't let the beige coats get you. Stay away from misery, from death, "Treat yourself," she says. *Buba,* your Nana Helen has spent her life eating fry-ups, chips, roast dinners and take-away food. Congratulations. *Kenahora.* "Celebrate," she says because death is obligatory, and death comes to us all. We must make the most of life, eat the ice cream, enjoy the Glories. But no one warned me, a child could be born and die. Perhaps if I had listened to my mum I would have understood. Perhaps I would have lit candles, baked cakes, kept coupons, laughed, and danced. Perhaps I would have said it when Antton and I first kissed: *kenahora.*

In my final year at university, Rachel and I bought my first computer on the Tottenham Court Road, in a shop selling cut-price hi-fi systems, next to the Scientologists Centre. "Look." Rachel pointed at a poster on the Centre's wall. "The Scientologists think death is not a worry as the spirit gets another body. But you have to be responsible for what goes on today as your spirit will experience it tomorrow. We're all immortal, baby!"

We cracked up laughing. Death was final. Death didn't mean anything. We were twenty. Death was so far away.

The first email I got on the computer was from Antton and he wrote,

An uncle of mine is dying, and I am going back to my mother's country for the funeral. We are in mourning. In the Basque tradition death links us all. Like veins. Or the mountain streams that come down from the Pyrenees, death is constant flow...

His message glowed on the computer screen: *Deceased. Burial. Land. Ancestors. Remembrance.* Antton—in what I told Rachel was "proof of his love"—took me to his Basque village, and I return to that trip, circling those days. It was the first time I had seen mountains. They overwhelmed me.

"You are young!" Katixa frowned slightly when she saw me, and before I left (I haven't mentioned this yet) she took me to their church. Inside, she walked away, knelt, lit a candle, and prayed. Antton said in a low voice,

"That precise square metre of the church belongs to the ancestors of our family house, the *etxea;* whoever lives in the house must pray at that spot. It is our household site on the church floor and called a *sepulturie.* We are expected to come to this *sepulturie,* kneel, light a candle, and celebrate all the dead people who have lived in our house."

Your grandmother, Katixa, never got to pray for you.

If she had been there when you died, I know she would have opened windows and removed roof tiles so that your soul could squeeze between terracotta slates. *Buba,* she would have rung church bells and gone to her hives to inform the bees. Without waiting, Katixa would have ordered and sent printed mourning cards indicating the place and date of your passing. The same day, she'd have done as the other Basque do, and put announcements in the monthly newspapers sent to Basque people in the United States, Latin America and Australia with the date and time of your Mass.

The next day, Katixa would have collected money from family, neighbours, and friends to buy good-quality salt, to be placed in the bowl and at the altar and distributed among the mourners. She would have told people not to wear black clothes as children were pure beings, innocent souls. She would have removed her mourning cape, put blue ribbons in her hair. She'd have provided bread and candles, so you would have food, and light to illuminate your way. She would have prayed for you, and I am calling her now.

I am asking Katixa, pleading her to come, before it is too late, to come and do all this, inside these notebooks: get the beeswax, light the candles, collect the bread and salt, call the mourners, take off the black capes, let the women walk by your body, let them weep and carry light to help make your passage safe.

Buba, as my final months at university ended, instead of studying, I spent my nights composing love letters on my computer and thinking about the sea. For hours on the phone, I chatted with Miguel about art and ignored my revisions. Instead, I pored over maps of the Channel, learning its contours and sea areas by heart and remembering the spot where I had met Antton: Hurd's Deep. When I graduated in June, I had been predicted a 2:1 or a First, but something strange happened, and I could no longer concentrate. It was like a small splintering.

Looking back now, I wonder if I was frightened about the future, if I couldn't face growing up. To everyone's surprise, I got a Third and decided to move to France with Antton. He was my beautiful escape, my alternative to a graduate job, marriage, a suburban life, to a future that I would now describe as beige: a bland stifling of everything. When I left for Paris, I thought our life together would be multicoloured, filled with laughter, books, baguettes; wine, and romance. He said, "Only a couple more years in this city and then I am leaving for the countryside." Antton wasn't sure that we should move in together. But I was twenty-one and told him, "It will all work out." He was worried about our age gap. I was carried by the sea, by the waves and my love. I apologise for my foolishness. But I will not apologise for my love. I repeat that, I apologise for my foolishness. But I will not apologise for my love. Do not say I told you so. It was a disaster.

5. What the Bee Knows

At 2:30 p.m., it was time for my afternoon therapy group, "Get Up. Get Out." Usually, the group "got out," walking in the grounds. They told us the objectives were motivation, motor skills, and stimulating interpersonal skills. What I liked was the retracing of a path, the gentle loop, the seasons changing. Today, at the start of session, Agnes asked, "What is today's date, day of the week?" evaluating time perception.

I couldn't answer, I had lost my sense of time and was steeped in thoughts of the funeral. Brutal and invasive. I replied I was looking forward to seeing the tulips growing in the grounds. Flowers emerging. But Agnes said, "It is late April. Today, for the Getting Out group, we're going into a café." Seeing the shock on my face, she commented, "Madame, you have been in the hospital for over two months. It is important you change environment."

In town, I didn't want to get out of the bus. I was scared to be outside, terrified of the road and the passersby. I was worried a car would skid and crash into our group, and what if I died, what if I didn't get to see you again, *buba*? Trembling, I kept looking over my shoulder, and when we finally got to the café and ordered drinks, Agnes came to see if I was all right.

"I grew up in London. I have been around noise and chaos all my life. I don't understand what is happening to me?"

She said it was the shock, and the staff often told me the same thing, as if this word SHOCK would provide relief. But their rational explanation didn't help. Recently I had discovered the bees were suffering from shock, their resilience was fading as the planet's heat levels rose. In severe heat, male drones convulsed, imploded, and died. Red lists produced by commissions proved these worrying facts.

In the bus, travelling back, I was red-faced and sweaty. Yann sat beside me. "I am making plans!" He said he was ready, whatever that meant. I wondered: was I ready? Could I go on a journey? What could I do about this shock? My inability to be outside the hospital walls. Was the environment unfriendly? What if the bees' disaster was linked to mine?

Yann said it would soon be the right time to travel on his boat. "The planets are gathering in the sky. A herd of planets." Jokingly, I told him that the planets were like swarms of drone bees, and Queen bees mated at fifty metres above the ground. The aerial congregation areas—where the male drone bees grouped—were at the height of the Tower of Pisa.

That evening, I wrote in the notebooks:

Drones only live twenty days but locate congregation areas as early as their second flight. Bees know the right place, the exact spot in the sky to fall in LOVE. But this is anthropomorphising. Bees do not fall in love, but from birth, they know their destination. I can tell you some of my love story, buba, as my love is your fate.

Buba, I need to explain: lots of love stories begin with non-love, half-love, something in-between. Love is not like the movies. It is not pastel coloured. Love is swirled crimson. Stripes of black gleam with a silver hue. It shouts sharply like shattered triangles of purple, and is turned sideways by a yellow tinge. Love is warm, in full brightness as the orange of papaya and sometimes grey and blurred, flattened by a middle tint. Then perhaps it is out of date. Ripe love is made of friendship, adoration, and sudden, vicious, boiling hate. It blazes on the open eye.

Love is like the story a Viking king once told of a swallow flying from a snowstorm into a banquet chamber through an open window. The swallow crosses the room, the table is laden with food, a warm fire is burning. The swallow flies out of the window on the other side, back into the snowstorm.

Love is ephemeral. Love is the swallow. Love is the room. Love is the fire. Love is the snowstorm. Love is long. Love passes so quickly you barely see. Love flies.

Buba, I admit, I didn't always love your father. When I fell in love with Antton what I loved was what he didn't show, what I imagined was behind the surface. Did I fall in love with the idea, the image I had of him? It is often like this when we fall in love, and we get to know the person afterwards. Either the image we had of them was correct and we love them even more, or they are different and our love is nourished from surprise. Sometimes, we dislike the new idea and our love is over.

When your papa and I first lived together it was not a great success. He walked out on me the very first day. It was late August, Paris, I was beginning an MA course at Paris 8 University; Antton had moved out of his Belleville flat. It was being sold, and despite his reticence, I had persuaded him to move in with me. It would be an adventure, and spontaneity was part of our love. *Live with me!* I emailed him, *Let's do the impossible.* In every life, we live through myriads of seconds, yet it only takes one to cast our world into turmoil.

"There are too many boxes," Antton kept muttering, as we marched up and down the six flights of stairs to reach our Marais *chambre de bonne.* My mum had sent me off with saucepans, mixing bowls, a kettle, and paper towels, "Because the French aren't always clean." She had packed Tupperware boxes filled with food for "while we settled in." Chicken soup, baked rice, sandwiches wrapped in tin foil.

"It's ridiculous. What are all these things for?" Antton had put most of his belongings into storage, and had two suitcases and a single cardboard box.

The tiny studio flat had a sofa bed, a kitchen area in the corner, and a minuscule bathroom. It was a sublet from a friend of Aunty Deb's. The tenant was a Liverpudlian tailor, who I suspected had a double life, living between Paris and London selling bespoke suits to Russian men. Once we'd filled the flat with our belongings, we could barely move.

As I tried to unpack, Antton looked out over the grey sea of rooftops, his shoulders hunched. I came to know that hunch well, along with his bitten bottom lip. While I unwrapped cups from newspaper, I asked him, "Are you OK?" but he didn't answer and the frustration grew inside me. You see, *buba,* when you love someone, you must learn their language as though it is a foreign tongue. Early on, I was not yet fluent in Antton's dialect and he didn't speak mine. I hadn't learnt that he was totally impractical. He didn't know about my moods. I hadn't got used to the fact that Antton was contained, a restraint that confused me. My childhood home had alternated between silence and noise, but Antton held his pain inside.

In the flat he tripped over a packet of toilet roll and snapped, "Anna, this is ridiculous. Get rid of some this stuff!" Blushing, I snapped, as I had often done with my mum,

"Don't tell me what to do!" Antton looked shocked, and I realised he'd never seen me lose my temper, and he told me to stop behaving like a child. I shouted at him that if he didn't like it he was free to leave, and he flung on his beige trench coat. Tightening the belt, he looked me in the eye, "You are impossible," and left.

Furious, I began stripping Sellotape from cardboard, opening boxes, pulling out paper balls, notes from my mum: instructions on how to make my favourite pearl and barley packet soup:

Empty contents of packet. Add 750ml of water. Simmer for 45 minutes. Enjoy this special homemade flavour. Our Edgware home erupted into the Marais flat. It felt pitiful. After a while, I found a box with a kettle, then discovered I couldn't plug it in. British plug. But I came across a Tupperware filled with what my mum called "diabetic cookies": parcels of puff pastry filled with currants and low-sugar jam.

Hunched over a box of books, with my mouth stuffed with pastry, I wondered what I had done. Everyone had warned me against moving in with Antton. He was too old. I was too young. I considered ringing Miguel—the only one who had supported my decision—and asking him to come and pick me up. Miguel was staying with my mum again. He was studying and putting together his first exhibition. "I will become a painter," he'd told me before I left. "Like you Anna, I am going to follow my dreams."

Two hours later, when Antton came back, I'd finished the biscuits. He walked into the flat and I stroked his cheek. He said, "We need to talk. But calmly."

Your papa often said this, *buba*, and he still says it now. Talking calmly is what he thinks we should do, talk about strategies, relationships, and memorials for you. Antton does his talking calmly, as though he is typing and each character lands evenly on the page. The only time I saw him lose it was when he tried to chop down the fig tree. It was late December, and in the garden his hands bled, and he was covered in mud, mud on his face, mud on his clothes. He lost control. "I can't get the tree to fall," he kept on saying. I held him in my arms while he wept.

Normally, when I shout, he becomes even calmer, and I shout more. When I was in the hospital, he no longer wanted to talk about you. He said,

"I can't do that anymore. My therapist says we each have our own work."

He wouldn't talk about what we could have done to prevent your accident. He wouldn't talk about how to bring you back. He refused to talk about the beige coat or the fig tree with the thin branches and the dark green leaves that he tried to cut down. "It doesn't make any sense," he said. I wanted to talk about your funeral, but I couldn't find the words.

That first autumn in Paris, we fought and worked, made love and rowed. Antton was tidy and I was messy. He could cook, and I preferred to eat crisps which he said weren't "real food." I could mend things, but he could barely change a light bulb. His bookshelves fell down, and I put them back up. He ignored me and read books on Lacan. He liked socialising, and I refused to talk to his friends.

In the winter, when we went out to bars I would sit and not utter a word, and the silence spread from inside me, until Antton's friends complained. By the spring, Antton and I argued so much the neighbours knocked on the door and asked us to be quiet. Anything sparked us off: he thought I was a slob because I left my dirty knickers on the floor, and didn't wipe the kitchen surfaces, or rinse the sponge. I found him a snob because he only liked highbrow books, and he frightened my mum who'd left school at fourteen and believed Antton to be "So. Clever. He. Is. Posh." According to Antton, only financial aspiration mattered to my mum, as she was saving up for a Mercedes. "You're simplifying her," I told him angrily when my mum came to visit for a weekend, and he sneered when she asked to eat onion soup on the Champs-Élysées.

By May, the heat in the flat was terrible, and we fought, had sex, and then fought again. Our only escape was to walk the Parisian streets and try and find fresh air. Crossing the Seine, we'd head toward the Jardins des Plantes or the Arènes de Lutèce. From the shaded steps, we watched women chatting and families playing badminton. Antton told me scraps of stories about himself,

"It is important for me to see people. I didn't have many friends when I was a child. I spent my time alone: reading and riding my bicycle. My mother told me not to talk to people. She didn't trust anyone in our council flats. One summer during the holidays, I made a friend, a neighbour's daughter, and we played together every day. Then in September, I found out she was in my school. And, in the playground, on the first day back, I pretended I didn't know her and that we'd never met, and to this day, I don't know why."

"People can be unreliable, even myself," Antton said. It felt like he was scared. Antton had grown up an only child in southwest France. Katixa (your grandmother) worked evenings cleaning office blocks. His father had passed away. At nights, he'd wait, "listening to the clock, and the neighbour shouting at his wife next door. I was stuck between the shouting and the ticking. Every night, I was terrified Katixa would not come home."

As we walked back to our flat from the Arènes, Antton said, "She made me work hard, said I had to pass exams and get a good job. She said life didn't offer any favours."

By June, even our evening walks were not enough. Antton told me that he loved me as dusk light reflected sweetly on the Seine but there was a permanent tension. We began to fight physically. I admit this to you, *buba,* as it didn't last long, for I said "Enough," and Antton said, "*Assez*" and left. In the flat, I began to cry, and strangely, after a day, I found I couldn't stop.

I rang Miguel. "It's all gone wrong," I said, "very wrong." Miguel borrowed my mum's car and took the Channel tunnel to Paris, packed my boxes, and took me back to London. I missed my final exams. Never got my MA. Antton left me a note saying he was sorry, that he would never forget me and that he loved me like he loved the mountains. Infinitely.

In Edgware, my mum welcomed me with fish and chips. The fish was fried in matzo meal and served with Russian pickled cucumbers. Aunty Deb sent me a card from Spain, quoting Blake: "The errors of a wise man make your rule." But I felt like I had completely failed. "You're home darling," my mum told me.

Bees and changing nests:

Over 70 percent of bees build their nests by digging in the ground. Most of these bees live alone. Soil is the most common material used by bees for nesting. Female ground nesters dig with their mandibles and "bulldoze" soil with their abdomens. The population of alkali bees in Washington can move almost 96 tons of soil in a year. Ground-nesting bees sometimes build close to one another, forming a group of individual nests called a "nest aggregation." Bumblebees do not reuse a nest. They change. Every year the Queen bee selects a new nest site and starts a new colony.

Back at home, after several weeks of lying in bed and watching old Lady Diana documentaries, my mum said,

"You're going to have to pay for your keep."

At first I refused. I wasn't ready, and I didn't want to go out and face the world and admit I'd been wrong about Antton. I was sad but I was also stubborn and stuck my feet in the sand.

I was headstrong as you were, *buba*. From age three, you would argue about not brushing your teeth, not wearing trousers that had an itchy waistband. "Too scratchy, Mama. TOO SCRATCHY!" you shouted, and you shouted later about bedtime, getting up and going to school. Your Nana Helen said it was your age, but it never changed, and at four you single-mindedly taught yourself to read.

In the kitchen at La Place, Antton shook his head, "You two are so single-minded. You'll stop at nothing!"

After Paris, I had to find something to do, and it was Miguel who gave me the idea of teaching English, because he said I loved languages, had a French degree, and,

"You can make some cash and will enjoy hearing the beautiful, broken, made-up, mispronounced speech. GFI!"

I got a Cambridge qualification and started work in a Central London language school. My job consisted of teaching grammar, pronunciation, phonetics, phonology, and conversation, QCM, true and false. Role plays. Job-seeking vocabulary and how-to-use-the-phone. Write emails. Formal and informal greetings. Beginners. Intermediate level. Advanced. Teaching the students how to pronounce the fricative English "th" sound, which is "soft, soft, soft," I said, "but lip configuration may vary depending on phonetic context."

Evenings, I went on blind dates, set up by my mum's friends, and didn't meet anyone I liked. My mum and I went on weekends to Bournemouth and walked by the sea. As Aunty Deb had developed a fear of flying, we tried to get to Spain at least once a year. Miguel graduated from Saint Martin's School of Art and went to live in Barcelona. He sent me handmade postcards painted with blue faces and orange smiles. He wrote on the back, *If you place one colour next to another they sing, and no one knows why. GFI!* At weekends, I saw Rachel, who was training to be a doctor at St. George's University. She lectured me on love and instability, and the role of serotonin in my life.

"You need to get your brain function balanced," she said, and told me to take Prozac instead of swiping Xanax from my mum. Rachel was specialising in neuropsychiatry, to understand "the machine that is the brain." As she predicted, following *How-To-Meet-Your-Perfect-Man in 5 Easy Stages,* she had fallen in love with a scientist, an entomologist working on pollination. She and James got engaged. He studied insects, and she focused on humans.

Miguel travelled and showed his paintings, in group exhibitions and then alone. His paintbrush rushed over canvases: condensed blue, yellow-red, and apple green. He became a successful artist, and fell in love with different men, finally settled for a wealthy Italian. They hopped between European countries, clubbing and dining and visiting galleries. He wrote in an exhibition catalogue:

The painter Chagall said colours are the friends of their neighbours and the lovers of their opposites.

It was one month since I had split up with Antton, two, three, four, five, six, seven, eight, and nine, twelve, and then twenty-four months and three years passed. I knew Antton still lived in Paris and worked at a lycée, near La Défense, and I thought about calling, but Rachel had told me I was NOT ALLOWED! Instead, I joined a book club filled with single women in their twenties, but I was bored by the over-sweet hot chocolate and dating talk.

It felt like I was walking in someone else's shoes, and what I was doing did not belong to me. Often, I wondered whether my fate was to live this unengaged dreary existence. Looking back, I think about Heidegger's *Dasein*, and I wrote in the notebooks:

Dasein—I've understood, in part, as discerning how we can be present in life. The word "Dasein" means "to be there" in German. Life is unpredictable and may not make sense. But we have to find what makes us feel with-the-world: like I did on the ferries, with books, and living with you and Papa. This being with-the-world feeling brought me happiness, and a sense of anchoring, a confidence I could win the fight. For, buba, life is a battle against beige. When I was living in London I was beige. When we are beige we are outside and not with-the-world. When you left I was outside. I floated, untethered, far away from life.

Summers, during my time off from teaching, I worked on the ferries and these weeks of freedom were my saving grace. Late

June, I counted down the days until I embarked, left the land and set out for the sea. Sometimes I worked from five until midnight. It was demanding. But I needed to be on the boats, and when the customers were aggravating and the sea was choppy, I learnt to walk through the door marked *Staff Only* into a calm haven; this small room felt like a privilege.

When we crossed Hurd's Deep where I had met Antton, I would glance at the red journey tracker and wonder where precisely things had gone wrong. My relationship with the sea never changed. Softly, calmly, it's immensity tapped at my life. On the shore, I listened to the sound of the waves breaking on the pebbles, swirling and regrouping; the noise gathered like a heartbeat.

In November 2005, I took a class of Chinese business students to Paris. We were in La Défense, on the main square next to the giant brass sculpture of a thumb. I was explaining to the students about the creation of the business area, the skyscrapers, when I bumped into a man. He wore a coat I recognized. The colour. The cut. "*Excusez-moi.*" He turned and gasped,

"Anna?"

"Antton?"

He hadn't changed much.

We stood as skateboarders did tricks on flights of stairs, flipping between hard ground and air, from safety to danger. He told me he was finally leaving Paris for a job in the South, "I only have ten months left in the city," and that Katixa had died the previous year. Teenagers in tracksuits somersaulted between concrete ledges while I offered my condolences. I asked about the house, but he said it had been passed on to a cousin. He was suddenly silent, and to change the subject, I told him about teaching in Central London with students from Japan, China, and Brazil.

Buba, what can I tell you? Fairy tales do not exist, but order was re-established. Three years of separation trickled between our fingers like sand. We both began to apologise for what had happened in Paris and then stopped. Everything belonging to the past disappeared. Cupids flew around the skyscrapers. Bells tinkled merrily above our heads.

If there is one thing I have learned, *buba,* love is what makes life worth living. For cynicism bites and gnaws at our hearts. It diminishes power whereas love is energy, and love is hope. As we looked into each other's eyes, one of the skateboarders rode into me, and I tripped and fell, banging my head on the pavement. I passed out, and when I came to Antton was peering at me anxiously. An ambulance crew placed me on a stretcher.

"*Ca va*?" he said, and it all began again as it had on the ferry. His "*Ca va?*" led to another. Once I had been discharged, for I had no serious injuries, we spent that night together in my room in a cheap Montreuil hotel. The following morning, breakfast was served on a plastic tray: bland jam in little portions, bitter coffee, and stale bread. Both of us had to leave early and we said hurried goodbyes, promised to keep in touch; we kissed awkwardly. I thought I would never see him again.

"What?" Rachel screamed, when I told her what had happened. "You're insane. I mean not clinically, but he's trouble. I am saying this for your own good. Remember when you fell in love with him before... Sometimes, I wish you'd never met him. I mean maybe you would have worked harder on your degree, not run away from that Paris MA. You've lost time over him. Don't do it again." She sighed.

When I texted Miguel, he sent back the word *LOVE!*

But Rachel was my oldest friend, she wanted my best. So I didn't ring Antton, or answer his calls, even though he tried to contact me. A month passed, and then a fortnight. My period was late, and I discovered, following a test, that I was pregnant. I was twenty-five years old. You had begun, *buba*. Everything changed.

In the hospital, I continued to write every night. Mornings, the nurses persuaded me, "Madame, you need to get out of bed. Take your sunglasses off. It's time for your therapy, your appointments." Exhausted, I often didn't reply. Finally, I saw the social worker, who explained, "You are in debt. It says here you spent nearly five thousand euros getting cameras installed and your locks changed at La Place?" I nodded. Most of the time, I was silent.

In May, the psychiatrist, Dr. Vidonne said to me,

"Madame, with all respect, I think it might help you to address what has happened. It is very difficult to lose a child. We need to help you work through your trauma but also your grief." She gave me a leaflet about: Shock and denial. Pain and guilt… Anger and bargaining… Depression… The upward turn… Reconstruction and working through… Acceptance and hope.

"I'm working through," I told her, while I skim-read the pages. It was a lie, but I didn't know what to say, for it was in my room where I believed the real work began. At nights, I continued my research, writing down all the names of colours close to beige, light tints of a neutral or pale warm shade:

Buff, Burlywood, Camel, Café au Lait, Dark Tan, Desert, Dirt, Ecru, Greyish Tan, Fallow, French Beige, Light Taupe, Lion, Mode Beige, Pale Brown, Pale Sandy Fawn, Raw Umber, Sand, Sand Dune, Shadow, Tan, Tuscan, Vegas Gold, Wheat.

I discovered the first time we heard of "beige" was in 1887, in the novel *La Fille Elisa*, the story of a young prostitute, by Edmond de Goncourt. In this moral tale, the fairy tale trio of colours appeared: red, white, and black. Beige slid into the book discreetly, describing raw wool and fabric neither bleached nor dyed. Alongside this fact, I scrawled other notes:

It is important to know that the military are often dressed in beige, khaki, also known as "drab." Beige is a colour of the modern world: frictionless, smooth, hard, and flat. Near-white is the colour of non-commitment. It is love without love. It is war without war. This colour annihilates the existence of colour. Beige entered our vocabulary when no one was looking. It sneaked into our world, invading our chromatic stage. It is death without death.

Then, I wrote this:

I have been in the hospital for three months. In the past few weeks, when I wake up in the mornings, it comes back. It will not stop. The funeral parlour visit. Is this what Dr. Vidonne calls "the flashbacks"? The funeral director wore a beige suit. He opened the door, and said, "Come in." The smell of beige, something chemical and sweet. He gave us options, "Burial, cremation, and/or burying ashes?" On his face was the dread of the dead child. You could not be associated with this dread. Lou and dread. You are/were funny, small, alive. You couldn't be here, and I couldn't either so I would not speak and didn't cry, and wished that I could disappear. We chose cremation and burial of the ashes. Antton and I chose what would be best. As if there was a best. The funeral director looked at me. He stared, and I almost laughed.

Until May, I barely spoke during my appointments with Dr. Vidonne, and sometimes after five minutes I left, but as tulips flowered in the hospital grounds, I found myself talking. It started with a book from the shelves of the hospital library: *The Secret Life of Bees*. One evening, I began reading it and I couldn't stop.

"It's extraordinary. I mean—" I said, before I had even sat down. I needed to tell her. "I read that all these different cultures, throughout time: Egyptians, Greeks, Romans, Hindus, Chinese, and others put pots of honey next to their dead. Like pots of gold or nourishment? There are even rituals where on the anniversary of a death, honey is poured over a grave."

And then I recalled what Katixa had told me that day in her kitchen, and how I kept returning to the bees and how they even came into my dreams. When I looked up, Dr. Vidonne was nodding. To be honest, I couldn't tell what she was thinking, but the following week, I continued: "I just found out Victorian families used to tell their bees about death, and they'd drape their hives with a black mourning cloth." I could scarcely believe what I'd read. "I mean, I knew about the Basque bee rituals, but the Victorians thought if these steps were not taken the family were not only putting the hives at risk, but without these precautions, death would take their whole family."

Our sessions continued, and the more I talked about bees, the more Dr. Vidonne smiled. She never said anything directly, but she was like a hunting dog that has caught the scent, and I sensed she was encouraging me, and things were making sense: the women, the honey, the wax, and the light. My knowledge of bees was merging: science and myth. Links had been broken, disaster had struck insects and human beings, bees and boys.

"Perhaps in this age," Dr. Vidonne said, "what we need to learn about is the best way to live through endings."

"I never knew this was happening all over the world. The bees are with us constantly, like they flew through time," I exclaimed during another session, "When archaeologists excavated ancient Egyptian tombs, the honey that they found inside was unspoiled. Did you know many societies have used honey to embalm corpses? But—" I paused, because I suddenly recalled that the bees were dying *en masse*, and death was slipping, once again, into our bee conversations. It was invasive, relentless, and I wondered what humanity would do without the bees? I had learnt that the bee was a symbol of life and I wanted it to remain that way. In Celtic languages words sounding like bee—in Cornish *"beu,"* in Irish *"beo,"* in Welsh *"byw"*—can all be translated as "alive."

The flashback. Early morning. I wake sweating and trembling. I feel like I can't breathe. Eight months since you died. The cremation, then the burial of the ashes. The cremation: the walls were beige. Huge empty beige expanses. They told us we could bring photos, but we didn't. We didn't know how to choose. They said we could select music, but we didn't. Instead, we said "Yes" when the funeral director proposed "something calm and neutral." There was a flat screen TV, and people spoke. In the background, photos were played on repeat. A beige sea, beige waves lapped on the shore. A beige sky. Wave after wave of beige. The teacher from school spoke and my mum spoke. Antton spoke. I didn't speak. I was drowning in beige and "sweet" and "lovely" and "missed" and "tragedy." The funeral director. Suffocated in beige. Sat on beige. Fawn velvet cushions. Cream chairs. Tissue boxes placed beside us. Walking through beige. I remember all of this. It doesn't change.

I remember:

It was July. At La Place. *Buba*, you were five. By the path to the house, the bees flew in the lavender bushes.

You asked, "What are the bees doing, Papa?"

"They are getting nectar from the flowers to take to the hives at Devant-La-Place."

"But do they sting the flowers?" you said, and Antton explained they didn't, and you looked relieved. Rachel was visiting with her husband, James, the entomologist. "These are our sunflowers," you told our visitors, pointing at the yellow heads. "There is one for Papa, one for Mama, and one for me." Behind the sunflowers, the fig tree cast shadows across the grass. It was heavy with green figs, and I remember wondering how the thin branches coped. James said,

"Well, do you know that flowers need bees, and that bees need flowers? Flowers and honeybees have evolved to need each other to survive."

You turned to listen to the tall, pale Englishmen. James looked like his limbs had stretched during adolescence, and he had never outgrown this coltish silhouette. He was kind, socially awkward and relentlessly meticulous. An example had been that very morning, when he'd taken over two hours to get ready for a walk, folding waterproof trousers and handkerchiefs, packing his rucksack with care, slotting a camera into place, plasters and snacks, everything examined and organised.

In contrast, Rachel—in less than five minutes—dressed, showered, grabbed a croissant, shouting, "Stop obsessing! We are going to be late!"

In the garden, James crouched, folding his long legs, and he stared at the insects for a very long time.

"This female worker has four wings that move at 11,400 strokes per minute. She has five eyes," he said pointing to a bee, "and she knows exactly where to land on the flower."

"But how?" you asked.

"Bees see with ultraviolet light. If you place the flower under a UV-sensitive camera, you'll see there are shapes like arrows pointing to where the bees should land." He explained how bees caught pollen on the hairs on their legs, flew to other flowers fertilising them by transferring the male part of one flower to the female part of another. As your eyes opened wide, he explained how bees stored the pollen in specific comb cells to make nutrition for nurse bees, so they could care for new larvae.

They did this by making "bee bread." Rachel and Antton went back into the house to open a bottle of wine, but you and I were captivated. James stopped. "Am I boring you?"

"No," we said. "How do you make bee bread?"

He said it was a mixture of ingested pollen, honey and enzymes. *Buba,* you loved James's diatribes. When our friends had gone back to Britain, you told me about the "waggle dance." James had described how bees returning from foraging needed to share their location with the other bees. They used a complex series of steps.

"A bee boogie," you said.

James spoke with enthusiasm. "Each step of the figure-eight dance communicates information about the location. The length of the waggles shows the distance from the hive." He held out his arm. "But this is not all. The energy of the dance tells other bees about the richness of the food supply." James jumped up and down. "Also, by angling her body in a certain direction, like this," he bent his knees, "the bee tells the other bees the exact way to reach the food. Finally, as she ends her waggle dance, the bee shares the scent of the flowers to be found. Basically, the whole boogie is a source of information."

For the weeks afterwards, each night you did a waggle dance. Singing and humming, you summoned the bees, celebrated and praised them, as the Romans, Clovis, and Napoleon had done.

"I learnt in a quiz the other day that the name Deborah in Hebrew means bees. The same name for a prophet and an insect," my Aunty Deb cackled with joy. Shortly before she died, she came from Spain to visit us in La Place. I have a photo to prove it. We didn't see much of each other any more. Before coming, she wrote, *I'll be travelling by coach. Don't like being up in the air. I'll die if I take a plane.*

It took her over eighteen hours to reach us; she had to change at Barcelona and she bought freshly baked honey cake. In our garden, she sat in a deck chair, lips painted red, her skirt pulled up, tanning her eighty-year-old legs.

"I love a bit of sun."

Antton took a picture of us, Deb, you and I, with a backdrop of sunflowers, the fig tree, and the bees. Tea and cake.

Buba, it is obvious now I should have told the bees of your passing, should have tried to find a hive to mourn your death. Were you doing the waggle dance now, shouting "Mama, Mama," from the other side?

Every night, I tried to find you in my dreams. Every day, I thought about you when I opened my eyes. For months after you died, I inhabited a time that belonged to us. My time was your time. It stopped the normal flow. When you were born we had made time together. When your time stopped, my time halted. Even if all the people in the world said, "We will die for you," and I would have died for you, they say that no one can die our death. Everyone is the first to die in their own lifetime.

Perhaps I should have built a shrine. For shrines are not just made for remembering. When a dog goes missing, owners are advised to put an item of clothing down where it got lost, for the scent. At first light, dogs can be found sitting on this clothing. People think shrines are for the living to remember, but I think they are doors for the dead to travel back. In this way, shrines are gates, openings in time; the flowers, collected personal objects, and candles are passageways through which the dead can access life.

Perhaps these orange notebooks are my shrine? Perhaps I am writing your ceremony here. I need to give you a door. During our coffee break at the Centre Via Langues, Monsieur Kassar looks through his poems, crosses out words, and rewrites, muttering, "We are the speaking mammals."

Is language our grieving tool?

In the hospital, I wrote about death in my notebooks because the subject was too big for me to say out loud. It was impossible to tell the nurses, Dr. Vidonne, or the other patients. I wanted to, but I was terrified. It was as though if I said the words, death would triumph.

You see, *buba*, we all fight against death. It is the battle they say we will always lose. From the day we are born we are ruins, tumbling from crack to stone. Every minute from birth is demise. It is impossible to move backwards, and not to step toward our unknown end.

Yet, in the hospital, death was commonplace, and somehow this was a comfort and a relief. Among the patients, there were the walking drowned, the miraculous empoisoned, the resuscitated overdosed. Bodies had survived being crushed by trains, veins cut, limbs burnt. In the corridors, I met jumpers who had tried to fly from high windows and had survived to tell the tale.

"What's the point in anything? We're all going to die. Why are we shocked when loved ones pass away?" a young woman asked, in the grounds, by a magnolia tree. Pink blossoms flourished and petals swooned.

The Queen of France woman appeared from nowhere with a scarlet bow in her hair, exclaiming, "Because we love. My dear, love calls us away from everything."

Buba, death obsesses humanity. On the outside it seemed everyone ran from this predicament. They pretended death was an illusion, tricked themselves by working, making money, praying, watching TV, trying to fall in love, cook, paint nails, dye hair, write reports and construct tall buildings, collect objects, book holidays, make babies, or stay single forever. People would do anything to deny the fact that everything was ending. The waters would rise, and the planet would burn.

The bees would become extinct, and we would give birth to children who'd die.

In contrast, I thought the patients understood death, and it was not only us that had fathomed the deep. We were also joined by the best nurses, the understanding doctors, the good psychiatrists, and the man who cleaned our rooms. I could tell he knew death by the way he swept his damp mop over the floor and gazed into the sky.

Inside the hospital, we looked death in the eye. We had to, for in hospitals decaying bodies found their place, the delirious mind, and the reach for death. None of this was forever. One evening, a young woman drowned herself in a bath. For days afterwards, I couldn't breathe.

I remember this:

"I am going to tell you a secret." *Buba*, you looked up at me, pen in hand, you were crouched on the floor next to my desk, surrounded by felt tips and paper. I was preparing a class on the difference between the simple past tense and the past continuous.

"Mama," you were repeating (past continuous), "I have a secret for you."

"OK." I lifted my head from my keyboard (past simple). You sidled up to my chair, placed your mouth next to my ear,

"The secret is, you have to do a line," you whispered (past simple, you get the point). "The line don't stop. You don't stop the line. It's a secret." Lou, you handed me a strip of paper on which you had drawn a purple line. Five minutes later, you called again "Mummy, *Mama*." You returned to my side. "What is Golden Trevor?"

"Golden Trevor?" I asked, and then I corrected you. "Oh you mean golden treasure."

You looked at me, crossly. "No, Golden Trevor. What is Golden Trevor?"

Trying to find a reference point in your vocabulary, I told you, "Golden treasure is what you find inside a pirate ship, like necklaces, rings and crowns. Treasure is a rare and beautiful thing."

You walked away and returned to your drawing, talking to yourself, "Yes. Golden Trevor, Golden Trevor is like a secret."

I looked at the scrap of paper and your purple line. At my desk, I wrote on the side of my paper: *Golden Trevor is this secret I whisper in your ear. It is a purple line.*

In May, Dr. Vidonne mentioned to Antton, who told me, "Anna is getting a little better but she is still very fragile and has an issue with sleep." I wasn't sure what either of them was talking about. Most nights I barely slept because I was working, researching: Diana, beige, the bees, collecting information about obituaries. The nurses came and tried to persuade me. "Madame, you must rest." I nodded and turned out the light. Then, under the blankets, I wrote using a torch. In the daytime, if I could, I stayed in bed.

Soon, Dr. Vidonne warned that if I didn't stop daytime sleeping, I would have to go back to the closed ward. But my research obsessed me. At night, it was logical not to sleep, and write instead.

"You must sleep at the right time if you want to get better, come home," Antton insisted on his weekly visit. Inside I smiled at the idea of getting better, for the flashbacks had got worse. And I still couldn't cry. It was the ultimate sign of maternal failure.

It was pointless explaining to Antton but it was obvious everything must be reversed. It was the only way. If the bees and boys were being slaughtered, drastic action must be taken. Throughout time, carnival had celebrated sacred chaos, let the fool be king for a day. Juggling dawn and dusk, I was inverting time, staying up into the magic hours like an owl. Blindly, I flew through darkness.

"I will try to do better," I told Antton, lying.

"I want you to come home. Anna, I need you."

Antton's face was filled with sadness, and I almost gave in and said, "Yes." His grief was visible. Until now I haven't written about this, because his suffering broke my heart. It was a silent wave. A dull, constant pain, and hour after hour it washed over him, dug grooves into his face. I longed to smooth them away. Place my hand on his cheek. Utter a gentle "yes" and remember our love and that knowledge of finding the thing you never thought you'd find. But home was the last thing on my mind. Returning to La Place was not viable.

Keats wrote a poem about building a boat from death, described building a vessel from dead bones. When I read it I pictured an ark constructed from grief and melancholy. A mast like a coffin hauled into the sky, sails blown into movement from lamentations and prayers.

Once I'd discovered this poem I knew I had to leave. Nearly three months had passed since I'd arrived. The flashbacks were unbearable. Everything collided. For days I had been thinking about Orpheus, and I knew it was time. Over dinner, I told Yann I was ready.

"Camille. I've been waiting for this day. My boat, Little One Hold Tight, is in Brittany at the port in Audièrne."

I nodded. "I need to cross the Channel," I said, although what I meant was that I needed to get to the middle, for there I could meet the beginning and the end. Yann looked at his watch, pulled out his phone, dialled a number, and started talking to someone, and then someone else about arrangements, his boat, and a woman called Sylvie, money in an account. "We can pick up my car whenever we want," he said. He began describing running away from the hospital and climbing over the walls at night, whereas I had imagined telling Dr. Vidonne. Soon, I was swept up by Yann's ideas as though they were a wave and they rushed forward, again and again, calling out: escape, escape. The following morning, he knocked on my door and shook me awake.

"I've written everything down here." He pointed to his head and disappeared. We were leaving in two weeks.

6. Unearthing the Stone

Agnes handed me my post.

"It arrived this morning." She smiled, eyes soft beneath thick lashes. She still reminded me of Diana, and I thought about how we all carried echoes of each other, the sharp eyebrow curve of one person; the tenor voice of another; the taste for spring honey or oysters. Stuff transmitted across time and space. "Madame." Agnes waved the postcard trying to catch my attention. Apologising, I took it, and when I saw the handwriting my heart beat. A card from Miguel, in my mother tongue.

There were days when I missed speaking in English. I had fallen apart in a foreign language, translating myself as I collapsed. Occasionally, with Dr. Vidonne I spoke in English, like when I was unable to find the French translation for "stillness," not calm or immobile. "Since Lou has gone, I am still," I said, and there was something about the sound of the word in English that I needed to say.

The postcard from Miguel showed a picture of an ancient mural: a row of female figures in profile in orange and red. Underneath was printed: *Etruscan threnody.* Recently, Miguel had texted me to say he was going to Naples to research the Etruscans, a pre-Roman Italian civilization, and their tombs. He'd asked for my news, and I hadn't replied. He'd phoned and I hadn't answered his calls. It was simpler not to have to explain.

On the postcard, he wrote:

Dear Anna, I think of you so often. Miss you. At the Naples archaeology museum, I saw the Etruscan frescoes. This one shows a threnody, female figures singing an elegy to the deceased. You, and Lou and Antton are in my heart. I love you darling Anna. I'll call again soon. I so want to speak to you. Pick up! Huge hugs Miguel

I stuck the postcard in my notebook, and wrote underneath:

Etruscan—check. A threnody—check. In the mural—irreversible loss appears as continuity. Women linked together, singing arm in arm, unstoppable, even against death. Women like the Basque and Breton, carrying and looking after the dead.

This mural is orange and red. The colour "orange" existed in Roman times, but the word "orange" was not used for centuries, arriving with the fruit from China. Before, the English-speaking world called this colour "yellow-red" or "geoluread" in Old English.

Buba, I could write a song on the virtues of orange. In the white of the hospital room, my notebooks were a quiet flame. When I arrived at the hospital in February there was one, and by the end of June there were nearly ten. They grew in number, until there was an orange tower. During those five months, I wrote in notebooks of different sizes, some had blank pages and others were lined, but all of them were orange. Inside them, I wrote:

Miguel said Van Gogh painted orange moons and stars in a cobalt sky. He thought blue was impossible without yellow and orange. Van Gogh searched for broken colours.

Kandinsky claimed orange was healthy, radiant, and serious.

Lorca wanted his soul to turn the colour of an orange.

Gertrude Stein questioned the orange centre.

Bacchus, the Greek god of wine, lust, and delirium was often depicted in orange.

Goethe described the union of orange and purple as the maximum of coloured appearance.

Princess Diana wore orange on regular occasions: a peach polka dot jacket with matching pillar box hat, a stunning orange red, sparkly gown, a blush blouse and skirt with a blush wide-brimmed hat, a salmon tonal outfit and a straw headpiece with salmon fabric pom-poms, a pale orange archer-style hat with marabou detailing, a clementine sharply cut belted suit.

Poets, artists, lunatics, and thinkers have all questioned the orpiment pigment. It is linked to amber, the gold of the North. Orange-lovers understand the blaze.

Remember—the day after Antton and I first had sex, we saw the orange Rothko painting. In the catalogue there was a quote: "Red, yellow, orange—aren't those the colours of an inferno?"

Buba, you told me orange was what came after anger, you said it mixes in the head, and everything is better with orange.

I remember this:

We were an hour from Italy, on the French Riviera. We had rented an apartment on the outskirts of Grasse. The balcony of our pale peach building overlooked the urban sprawl falling from the mountains into the sea. It was your sixth birthday. We were driving along a serpentine road beside belle époque villas, baroque castles, and mirrored modern apartment blocks. All the buildings were orange, a coral glory bright against the green vegetation, contrasting with the blue sky and the blue sea. Peach facades, marigold walls, ochre and tangerine edifices, salmon orange close to pink, red-nearly-amber. Mopeds sped past, propelled by tanned teenagers. A scrabble of shops sold pottery, striped parasols, and inflatable crocodiles. On promenades, women's airy white dresses fluttered like sails. Everything led to the sea.

For your birthday we had bought you books, the purple T-shirt you wore, new felt-tip pens, and notebooks. "How was I made?" you asked from the back of the car; we had been talking about your birth, conception.

“Do you remember?” I put my hand on Antton’s thigh. “The Paris hotel.”

“Of course,” Antton replied and I smiled, as recently, in a private class for a university literary professor, I had been struck by the different uses of “conceive.” It could mean forming or imagining an idea, but also referred to the instant when life took hold. Perhaps conceiving a human was both of these, required a physical act and an imagining, a pouring of longings and wants into a future person. Secretly, I believed your conception had happened unexpectedly yet had tapped into the seam of our love. Without these longings could *you* have existed, or would you have been someone else?

On that sunny day on the Riviera, you brought me back to the present day, yelling, “What Paris hotel? Mama, Papa, what hotel?”

Antton and I tried to explain that this hotel was linked to where you were made.

“But how was I made?” you asked.

“Daddy put a small seed inside mummy.” We giggled.

“Very small?”

“The size of a crumb.”

As we walked toward the beach, you began asking a series of complex questions:

“How did I get out of the tummy of Mama?”

“Am I like a sunflower?”

“Did the bee help?”

“When can I have a Glory?”

Antton diverted your attention. He pointed his finger and your eyes turned.

“The sea. Look, Louis! We all come from the sea originally. Once we were all fish.”

“I was a fish, a fish, a fish. I want to swim, swim, swim! I love you. You are the best!” you shouted, and you ran into the water.

On the beach, we stretched out on our towels. You came and went, jumped and splashed, kid's limbs: poised and free. That summer you danced wildly as soon as there was music. You were fearless and more gregarious than either Antton or me. You talked to everyone. "My name is Lou." You stood, fierce, legs outstretched, like a miniature gangster from a black and white film. You imagined poems and drew with every colour from the palette.

On the beach, you dug a hole, and put your feet inside and sand on top.

"Mama, I'm hiding my feet. They have gone." You turned, eyes trusting. Behind you, turquoise waves crashed on the shore.

"Oh, you're burying your feet." I was not entirely listening, and flipped through the pages of a magazine.

"What is burying?" you asked.

"It is when we hide something or put something beneath the ground. Like treasure. Buried treasure."

"We buried Aunty Deb."

Frowning, I put the magazine down, wanting to change the subject. It was painful. Deb had died the year before, and her body had been flown back from Spain for a London funeral, her bare wooden casket in the grave. On the beach, you repeated, "We buried Aunty Deb. Can she come back?"

Antton had gone for a swim. Sighing, I wondered what to say. Recently, I had spoken to Rachel about how to talk to you about death. She'd said,

"You must know what Lou's brain is cognitively capable of and adapt what you tell him. Between three and five, children deny death as being final. They think it is a journey from which we return. Between five and nine, they understand death is final but think if they are clever, they can trick death."

Her advice was straightforward but I was still confused. Lou had questions but so did I. By now, Deb had been gone a year, but I still thought the phone would ring, and I'd hear her voice. I felt death had tricked me. Deb could return. On the beach, when you asked, "Can Aunty Deb come back?" Rachel's one-size-fits-all rational explanation wasn't enough. Something was missing: an invented ceremony, ritual. The previous evening, I'd talked to Antton about grief, and he'd said, "This is why we need art and music" and *buba*, when your papa spoke like this he opened a space in my godless heart.

Looking out at the waves, I answered, "We did bury Aunty Deb. We loved her very much, and—" reaching over, I placed my sandy hand on your chest. Beneath my palm, your heart beat in time with mine. "Aunty Deb is still with us, and she once told me the only thing that counts is how much heart people give, how boldly they run through life. If all of us think of Aunty Deb and hold her close, she stays with us. In our hearts. Forever."

You looked down and placed a stone in the sand. You sang and drew circles. "My feet are hiding and here is the key. My feet are buried. But, if you have the key you can find them."

Relieved, I returned to the pages of my magazine. On the beach, *buba*, you pressed a stone into my palm, and I felt its warm contours and I thought, we are here on the beach, it is your birthday. We are a family under a parasol. We will read books. Eat ice creams. Build sandcastles that will crumble. Later, we would stick candles in a Glory, sing "Happy Birthday" and you would blow the flames out. Our love would spill, uncontrollably, into orange evening light. The sea would always bring the waves to the shore. Nothing could tear us apart.

In the Consolation to Marcia, Seneca wrote that if we knew the harshness of the life in front of us, many people would not choose to be born.

Undertaker bees:

Undertaker bees clean the hive of carcasses, carrying out all the dead and dying bees. Sometimes they fly the dead and dying twenty feet away from the hive, dropping them to the ground. Other times, they haul out bees too big and heavy to be lifted into the air. This behaviour is called necrophoresis; it is a sanitary measure preventing infectious disease.

On the Internet, when I type "THE BEES ARE DYING" I get 11,000,000 results in 0.67 seconds. Currently, due to the state of the planet, the deaths are colossal and the undertaker bees overwhelmed. I wonder who will carry all the dead bees safely to the other side?

I remember:

Here is a list of the questions you asked in two languages. I write them here in English:

1. *What is the shape of the sky?*
2. *Can you taste blue?*
3. *Why do we speak English and French?*
4. *Where is my rabbit Lala?*
5. *What is after summer and after autumn, winter and spring, what is after?*
6. *How do babies get out of tummies?*
7. *Can I have more chocolate cereal?... Can I have more chocolate cereal?... Please, Mama...*
8. *Where are my granddads?*

You often asked this, Louis, when we talked about Nana Helen in London, and your Basque grandma Katixa who was dead.

"She's not in the sky," Antton said, "but she is in our hearts."

"Where are my granddads?" you asked.

You were like the students in my language classes, during first lessons, reading a photocopied sheet: "Where do you come from?" "To begin, let's start with father and mother." When you asked,

"Where are my granddads?" I couldn't answer precisely, because our fathers were not in our family picture frames. Unintentionally, we had removed them from our home, written them out of our lives. It was something Antton and I shared, an avoidance of our paternity, and when people asked: *What about your father?* We changed the subject and left a blank space on each administrative form. If we imagine that each of our answers was a stone, Antton and I piled our pebbles, rocks, and stones together until we had created massive forms like the *harrespil*, the Basque "stone circles," megalithic monuments found on mountain flanks. Our ancient structures were like all family secrets: they took a long time to build, were hard to demolish, and impossible to ignore.

"Where are my granddads?" you said.

Now, I regret that I did not undo our secrets, dismantle our closed rounds of stones, and tell you the truth. *Buba*, I should have shown you the rare photos of our fathers. Instead, I said, "I grew up with Nana Helen and it was lovely," and offered you a chocolate biscuit, and Antton answered, "Let's go outside and see the sunflowers," and he took your hand.

Some people are brave. They open their mouths, undo secrets that are centuries old. They topple statues and rebuild the foundations. People can change history.

"Diana spoke the truth about the royal family," my mum said after Lady Diana died. "She broke the silence and spilled the secrets on the BBC."

My *buba*, it is urgent I tell you about your grandfathers, the paternal branches on your family tree. Antton's father came from near Pau, worked on the family farm. He died when Antton was a baby and Katixa never mentioned him. One Parisian evening, Antton said, "All I know about my father is his death. His car crashed on a mountain road. My mother told me he liked driving fast. My father said what was the point of having a car if you couldn't taste the pleasure of speed!"

Following the accident, Katixa brought Antton up alone in France, left the family farm as, "I didn't get on with my mother-in-law." She cut all ties with Antton's father's family and was too proud to return to the Basque country. Instead, they moved to a town where nobody knew them, and Antton always longed for home.

As for me, my dad left my mum when I was born. She was a Londoner, he was not. He wanted to travel and she refused. "It was complicated," Aunty Deb said, for it was she who told me the story. When I was three, with Aunty Deb's help, my mother got a divorce. She had to prove that she had done everything in her power to find her husband, that she had contacted: Friends. Relatives. Last known employer. Banks or building society. Trade union or professional organisations. She submitted a legal notice in the local newspaper to serve her spouse. "Your dad worked as a diamond dealer, and he disappeared." Deb told me, "There is nothing more to say." Yet, his absence glittered, a tiny stone embedded in my rock.

My mother and I grew up together. "The two of us against the world," she said. With Aunty Deb we made a threesome, jumping through the waves. Then, I met Rachel, Cyril, and his Ferris wheel. On the ferry, I was eighteen and Antton and Miguel entered my stage. Louis, you arrived when I was twenty-six. We moved to La Place and lived at the end of a lost country lane. I learnt to put up plasterboard and tile the bathroom. "I miss the smell of London," I told Antton, and he laughed, but I wasn't joking. Outside in nearby hamlets, stray cats idled, and in surrounding villages the annual event was an Abba tribute band. I missed Miguel and Rachel, as I drove past streams, rivers, lakes, hedges, valleys, bushes, mud, sun and sky. I longed for the city, it's stink and hum, but for six years I made a home. You were there, and after you'd gone, Yann came to greet me in the hospital, and spoke to me about the "crack."

But *buba* I am not telling you everything, not yet.

Once Yann and I had decided we were leaving, I went to see Dr. Vidonne,

"I'm feeling much better. I'd like to go home for the weekend."

The psychiatrist examined me, as though I was a bubble in a spirit level, measuring whether I was crooked or straight. She said I could go home, but she wouldn't reduce my medication. "Not yet. Better to be safe than sorry." I sensed she knew something was up, and almost admitted I was planning a trip, which meant that things would change irremediably. Of course, I held my tongue.

Yann and I decided it would be dangerous to share our plans. However, I added, "It's like a weight has lifted from my shoulders," and I wasn't telling lies. Something had shifted. For months, I'd been stuck, powerless, veering in my light and then leaden state. All the time, I had been waiting. It was a wait for the patter of feet, the sound of your voice, for your hand to loop in mine. Time had stopped. But *buba*, once I took the decision to go with Yann, I pressed a button and re-started the machine. It meant a sequence of events clicked into place. I was leaving everything behind me, and I would find you, I had nothing to lose. Finally, I was free, and could jump over into the land of the dead. The future was irrevocable, and the consequences uncertain, but time flowed again. I had flipped a coin. Heads or tails, and if I fell, it would be forever. Yet it was a relief to know this was my final journey, and that I walked with Yann, the boatman, by my side.

When I had Dr. Vidonne's permission to leave the hospital for the weekend, I rang Antton. "Wonderful," he said, and a wave of guilt came over me, for I heard the happiness in his voice and knew that later, once he discovered I had left the hospital with Yann, he would not feel the same. The following Saturday,

Antton came to fetch me, and by late morning, we were walking around our garden at La Place. Antton told me he had made Basque cod stew, Katixa's recipe.

Buba, you loved to watch your father cook the fish stew. Dressed in a black apron, he chopped and fried onions and garlic in olive oil, added fresh or tinned tomatoes. Antton hummed as he worked. "Come on, Lou," he would say, "help me cook!" and he let you sprinkle salt, toss red paprika, a pinch of sugar, a pepper mill grind. The cod stew was baked slowly in a round terracotta dish, until the fish flaked, and the green oil shone.

In the garden at La Place, the scent floated in the air. It was sweet and fragrant. "You seem so much better," Antton said as we walked past the lavender bushes, the bees, and the fig tree. "They are blooming early this year." He pointed to the sunflowers. We held our breath, and neither of us spoke. Antton's hand slipped into mine, and out of nowhere, I wished for things to be different. I wished I'd never left for the hospital and had not been in the closed or the open ward. I wanted to delete the pages in the orange notebooks, cross out the loose-knit, desultory sentences on Diana, Orpheus, death, and remove the obituaries I had cut from newspapers, the victims of beige. Everything was insignificant, even my plans for the journey with Yann. I wished I wasn't going away. All that was left was Antton and me.

Glancing up, I saw the house at Devant-La-Place, the chickens. The sun caught the hills, the curve of land, the lake, and the deep water. Closing my eyes, I felt the heat on my face, and Antton's lips were on mine. We'd barely made love since you had died, and we rushed upstairs to our bedroom.

Between the sheets, we found each other again. We made love trying to catch up for the past months, and in the memory of other nights. We made love for the ferry, for Paris and for the lake. We soothed our bodies sore from grief, chased the mourning ashes from our skin. We made love for a future life that we tried to count on the fingers of one hand.

"*Extraordinaire. C'est le fil,*" Antton whispered as I lay with my head on his chest. It was a joke between us that there was an invisible thread, linking us together, a thin transparent strand of silk. When we were apart, if I tugged the thread, I would think of him, as though with this tiny movement I sent a love note to Antton, and wherever he was, he sent one back.

"We have the power of ubiquity," he whispered. His hands touched the hollows of my hips. Antton fell asleep. His chest rose and fell, and I began to cry. The tears trickled down my cheeks, without interruption, as though someone had turned on a tap. I hadn't cried for months. *Buba*, I hadn't wept. As I lay in our bed, I felt peace and terrible sadness, for I was going on a journey and there was no turning back.

The following morning, after breakfast in the garden, Antton drove me back to the hospital. As we crossed through the gates, he said,

"Please come home soon, Anna. I miss you terribly."

I nodded my head but couldn't answer.

I missed Antton too; I missed your father, *buba*: his smile, his gaze lost in the horizon, his ability to sift through contradictions, and find the right way to describe the familiar and make it unfamiliar, and the other way round. I missed the toast he made us for breakfast, spreading the jam evenly over each slice. I missed the black hair on his chest. His lean body. Slim ankles. His stories about the Basque country, and the way he expressed surprise, his mouth drawing a circle of naivety. His hands. His quiet fury at injustice. His high standards for cleaning. His impractical nature and inability to read a plan. I missed his mind, his heart, and his body close to mine when each day fell and the dawn came. Since you had died, I missed everything about him.

Buba, love is an intimate language, only spoken by the lovers involved. Each couple invents the nomenclature through which they live their joint existence. Their language is a boat in which they travel. A breakup is a shipwreck.

Once, when Miguel split up with a long-term lover, he emailed me,

The days are painfully, terribly slow. I've spent hours working on a plank of wood, following the grain with a tiny brush. I have abandoned all the colours and I don't know what to paint. This absence is, above all, an exercise in patience.

Buba, after you left, I missed Antton. For after you died, I did not just lose you, I also lost my man, my other half, my partner in crime. We were torn apart. When you died, I also lost your father.

7. In the Steps of Orpheus

The poet Etel Adnan wrote a new version of the Orpheus myth. She claimed the reason the gods didn't want Orpheus to look back at his wife as she climbed out of the world of the dead is because there was nothing there but total absence.

I find this idea so awful; I can hardly write it down.

"It will be much better that way," Yann told me after dinner, looking out of the window in my room. "We must run away in seven days, at midnight, under the full moon. The energy will be right, and the stars aligned. It is the Delta Era, and currently Pluto circles the outer rims. We need to begin with a radical cosmic act."

Yann began talking about the stars and fortunes, mixing astrology, astronomy and cosmology. "I know about the coordinates in the sky, I am a highly experienced skipper, can read minds, I trained at the *École Nationale de la Marine Marchande*." Not everything Yann said made sense, and he shoved a folded piece of paper in my hand, saying,

"I've made a plan, and drawn out two copies." When I opened it, there was what looked like a hansd-drawn fake banknote with a celestial map surrounded by gamma ray bursts. "Oh, that is for a different project." Yann snatched the note back and handed me a list entitled:

How to Get Camille to the Middle of the Channel:

1. *During the week before leaving, take extra baguette at every meal, portions of jam (a spare knife). Supplies are important for astral journeys.*
2. *Pack bags and try not to sleep. Insomnia helps cosmic forces in astrophysics.*
3. *Escape at moonlight over the easterly wall of the hospital. Remember to be orientated. This means face east, face the part of the world where the sun rises.*
4. *Collect my yellow 2CV car outside the hospital gates.*
5. *Drive overnight to Brittany, drive west-northwest. Travel by instinct, following azimuth to Finistère to collect Little One Hold Tight from Audièrne.*
6. *At high tide sail out to the middle of the English Channel, recalling the motto of the École Nationale de la Marine Marchande, "Obey to command." One must adapt to the wind and not the other way round.*
7. *Realign the stars.*

When I read the list, a shiver ran down my spine. I wasn't sure whether Yann was the right boatman, and I wasn't sure what he meant about realigning the stars.

"I need to get to Hurd's Deep, for Louis," I said quickly. "Add it to your list. That is our destination!"

Yann nodded and wrote it down. "We'll leave next week, on Monday. It should take us about eight hours to drive to Brittany."

In the end, we drove for three days.

Even now, *buba*, I know we didn't have to escape. Neither of us had been sectioned. We were in an open ward and not legally obliged to stay. We could have told the staff, the nurses, social workers, and our psychiatrists. It would have been easy to depart in broad daylight. Instead, one week later, at midnight, carrying my suitcase, I sneaked out of my room and edged down the corridor. In the staff room, through the window, I saw the night nurses talking, their faces lit from the computer screens. The dark-haired nurse was yawning, and Agnes was typing, she frowned in concentration. Looking back, I wish I had said goodbye. But Yann was beckoning to me to hurry up. He'd stolen the keys, and the lock creaked open before we slipped through the door.

Outside, the full moon lit the grounds, meaning we could find our way easily. When I looked back at the hospital, I thought I saw a figure at the window. The Queen of France woman was waving goodbye, I waved back, and then we walked down the path and climbed over the low crumbling east wall. It was simple. Easy as pie.

"People thought the east contained our original home," Yann whispered, "It is dawn, the start of light."

His car was parked around the corner from the hospital. I shoved my suitcase on the back seat. Inside were my chunks of baguette, portions of jam, and my orange notebooks, wrapped in plastic bags to protect them from water damage once we were on the boat. As I sat next to Yann, I felt happier than I had for months.

"I hope the car will start." Yann sounded anxious, and when he turned on the ignition, the engine spluttered, but then it purred. "We're off! Camille, we're on our way!" He turned left and then right, explaining he didn't have a map, "but I know the route back to Brittany off by heart."

Neither of us had GPS on our phones, and we left the hospital in a moment of elation, got lost, and then got lost again, until we were driving in the middle of the countryside, following bright yellow deviation signs. One of the car headlights was broken and we could barely see.

"I can't believe it!" Yann shouted as we rattled through narrow country lanes into the darkest night. "It shouldn't be this difficult." A wave of worry flooded over me; we'd been driving for nearly two hours. "Don't worry, Camille!" he retorted when I said, "Aren't we going round in circles?" Suddenly things got confused. Yann started muttering about stars and the subject of telescopes and Newton. I worried he was entering a manic phase. He had told me this happened when things went too fast.

"Maybe we should take a break?" I ventured.

"No fucking way. They're not stopping my freedom." Yann began swearing, saying all sorts of things, and I wondered if he had taken his medication, or whether he had decided, as he told me he had done in the past, "to let things roar." Yann had alluded to what happened when he didn't take his pills and "lost the plot," vague ramblings about things being "broken," a cousin he'd "hit," and a knife with "a very sharp blade." I wondered if I had made the wrong decision, if Yann was a dangerous choice, and I shouted, "Maybe we should go back?" regretting the words as soon as they were said.

Yann slammed on the car brakes, got out, and shut the door. We were in the middle of the road, in the middle of nowhere, and I got out of the car. Outside, Yann paced back and forth. It was quiet, and darkness surrounded us. Not a light to be seen, except for the moon. It hung in the sky, a giant yellow orb. All I could hear was Yann's shuffling feet, his breath as he inhaled and exhaled, and the sound of animals and insects in the undergrowth.

"Are you OK?" I whispered. He didn't answer and I knew better than to ask again. Then, he whispered, "Camille, Camille. Look!"

From the darkness, a stag had appeared. It stood in the middle of the road, in front of the car. Its antlers reached to the sky. Outlined in the moonlight, the stag faced us, staring. We waited and it seemed like the whole night waited with us, and the sounds of the undergrowth disappeared.

It was as though the stag possessed this lost lane, this nocturnal hour and this dark night. It owned the leaves, the mulch, moths, foxes, mice, voles, badgers, and bats. It owned all the living things, and the sky and the stars. The stag owned Yann and me. We all waited, and the inky, sloe-black grew denser, until the night was condensed, compressed into a velvet sable darkness.

Then, the stag turned and leapt, over the hedge, into air and brush. The stag crossed over to the other side. If I could have, I would have followed it, through the night. Aunty Deb had always told me to look for signs from the animals. The stag had opened the gates to the land of the dead.

When Orpheus went to get his wife back from Hades, at first, they would not let him in. At the foot of Proserpine and Pluton's throne, Orpheus knelt and tuned his guitar. His music vibrated in the underworld. He sang: "I plead with you in this terrifying place, in the silence of Night's pace, return Eurydice to me, reconnect the threads of our love's lace."

The shadows and the Manes wept for thirty-eight minutes. Ixion no longer turned on his burning wheel. Tantalus stopped following his shadow, and the vultures froze mid-bite of Tityus's intestines, which were spread, red and sticky, on a desert floor. They claim that even the inflexible Furies were shocked enough to shed a tear.

Together, they called to Eurydice, and she came from the underworld. But Proserpine and Pluton made a deal. "Orpheus, your singing has enchanted us. You can leave with your wife, but you must promise not to look back at her."

I wondered if Proserpine and Pluton would accept my orange notebooks (as they had accepted Orpheus's song), would this be enough to persuade them to open the door?

Neither Yann nor I moved or spoke. An owl hooted and flew across the sky. An alabaster billowing beyond the black. The sound of the insects and animals resumed. I turned to Yann,

"We need to get to Brittany and find your boat. In the middle of the Channel, I will find Lou." There was no turning back.

For the following two days, we continued getting lost, arguing, and finding our way. Due to the age of his car, we were obliged to use the *route nationale.* We were too slow for the motorway. To eat, we munched on the stale baguette (we had managed to steal seven pieces each) and then crept into fields and took melons or tomatoes. Neither of us had much money, and we had to keep filling up on fuel. Yann persuaded me to take out cash. "We mustn't use our bankcards. We could be traced by the police or the CIA. They will find us, and it will all be over. It has happened to me before." He told me to keep my phone off so people couldn't call, and he kept looking to see if we were being followed. "They may be recording our conversations and we must check the car for hidden microphones."

Buba, you may wonder why I believed what Yann told me, or at least why I didn't question his wild ideas. But I felt fearless and reckless, grateful things were finally moving, and all I could think of was you.

The sun was rising over broad rolling hills when Yann told me about his boat.

"You see, at the age of eighteen, I qualified to be a skipper. Top of my class at the École Nationale de la Marine Marchande. Then I sailed yachts for people around the world, crossing the Atlantic. As a captain, I was our clients' first port of call, and always available, amiable, alert in storms. I worked hard, and harder. Able to mend motors, fix each sail. Navigating in any kind of weather, I had a sixth sense; I could feel the storms. Day and night, I stayed awake, drank Coke and coffee, barely ate, nothing could stop me. Soon, I worked for luxury yachts, made a bunch of cash, and I bought my first boat, a yacht for ten, *Tiens Bon'* Hold Tight, but—" Yann looked at me. "I lost that boat because they pushed me too hard, I lost it and then they sacked me." He paused and breathed in. "I fell ill, was hospitalised for the first time. Like many sailors and fishermen, I had developed a cocaine addiction. And, then it was a yo-yo, I worked and fell ill, worked and fell ill, but I saved up, and a few years later I bought *Petit Tiens Bon,* Little One Hold Tight, the child of the first boat, and I moored her where my father had moored his first boat at Audierne port, in Finistère. I paid Sylvie to look after her. Sylvie is a pearl."

"Who's Sylvie?" I asked him. But Yann just muttered, "She's a pearl. You'll find out later." He shrugged. "Camille, I know I sometimes lose control. But even when I was young I knew I was not like other people. I will only admit this to you, Camille, but I have a power that is rare. I can sense people's moods from colours around their bodies. You, for instance," he tapped his hands on the steering wheel, "Camille, the first time we met I saw you were orange. You glowed, even before you started writing in those notebooks. You might have been broken but orange poured from each chink and crack. It flowed into the room. You burnt like a flame, and the thing about fire," Yann's voice slowed, "fire is not just about warmth or cooking. Fire is desire."

As I listened to Yann, I knew everything he told me wasn't true. But when he spoke, I wanted to take his hand and I would have run with him to the end of the earth. It was impossible not to follow him.

At the start of the journey, I continued having the funeral flashbacks. In the hospital they had been there when I woke up, but now it was any time of day. They came when we drove through the countryside and towns, past out-of-town shopping centres and gigantic industrial silver silos. The flashbacks emerged: a beige day. The undertaker. The suit. Screens. Television, pictures of pebbles. The sensation of being gagged. My mouth was sewn up and I wanted to call out, but the words wouldn't come.

Beige makes it seem as if the tremendous effort and energy that go into the movement of being alive don't exist.

That night we parked in a lay-by next to a vineyard. Grapes grew across each field, and in the distance a small château was perched on a hill. Yann took the back seats and left me the front. We had forgotten to bring bedding, but he found an old blanket in the boot.

"You can use it, Camille," Yann said. He looked after me, opened doors, and placed my coat carefully around my shoulders. He had an old-fashioned gallantry.

The following morning, after a two-hour drive, we were hungry, and our bread was stale but petrol was low and we had to save our cash. "We'll stop here." Yann took me into a grocery shop, grabbed croissants and bananas, shouting, "Camille run!" Without thinking, I followed him, and the cashier chased us out of the door. We jumped into the car, jubilant like a couple of outlaws.

It might seem odd, *buba*, but as the hours passed I felt stronger, like I was taking control and was in charge of my life. There were no rules, no nurses or doctors, no Antton telling me what to do and when. The flashbacks came and went, and I accepted them. After months in the hospital, it was as though I was finally free, and we could do anything.

As we headed north, we reached villages of chalky white low-lying houses. Their roofs tiled in red, a spark of colour, a dash of blood, and I thought of Frida Kahlo, who painted her own red horror onto canvas. I said to Yann,

"I saw her work at the Tate Gallery in London with Miguel. Tiny paintings, but it was like they grabbed you and Frida was shouting: *this is life.* She painted her body bleeding, her miscarriages, her pain, her dreams. During a childhood tram accident, a metal pole severed Frida's body. She knew about lives with two sides."

Frida Kahlo believed red was the oldest colour. The colour of blood and menstruation, and I remembered red seeped from me when you were born. But, *buba,* nothing seeped from me when you died, and I would have liked something to have come from inside me to show that you had gone.

This thought troubled me as we got closer to our destination, but not as much as Yann's behaviour. He seemed to unravel as I felt better. He had practically stopped eating, just drank coffee and Coke. "We'll be in Brittany tomorrow," he said, as we crossed through marshlands, past narrow waterways and low-lying bridges.

We parked near to what Yann called "the gateway to Brittany."

"In the morning we'll drive to the tip of the earth, to Finistère. One of the most beautiful places you will ever see. The light illuminates your soul and extinguishes dreams in one day."

He got out and began checking the car and scrutinizing the sky. When he wasn't looking, I turned on my phone. There were texts and vocal messages from Antton. Holding my breath, I deleted them. *Buba,* I must admit this. I didn't read or listen to Antton's messages. It would have been impossible to continue if I had heard his voice, I would have jumped from the car and said to Yann, "Stop."

How fast can you make honey?

Human beings have developed the culture of hives to make honey. They build boxes filled with empty frames and a removable roof. Bees are invited to set up home, often using a scent lure. Once installed the bees fill the frames with honey, pollen, and brood. On average it takes about a month for the hive to be ready for humans to harvest the honey. However, when the bee colony is particularly strong, and weather and environmental conditions are right, bees can fill a hive with honey in just a few days. Taking honey is a form of theft.

"Brittany is where I belong," Yann said, "but I am always scared of coming home." He said it was a land of druids, mystery, and silence. He said that druids used honey and that Pythagoras's mentor was a druid, and Pythagoras only ate honey. He told me Brittany was a peninsula, shaped like a horn, sticking out of the west side of France. I told him I knew the coastline, as I had worked on the Channel ferries. But Yann didn't seem to hear what I was saying. He was lost in his thoughts.

"Camille, you must understand the Breton soul. In Brittany the sea speaks to us from three sides. I should have been listening. Why did I never hear her wave song coming from the salty waters?"

Yann didn't sleep again that night, and when I woke the following morning he was outside, pacing round the car. His face was marked by bags beneath his eyes, and he beckoned to me to hurry up. He drove fast that day, and then faster, and finally, we crossed into Brittany. As we entered the region, memories of my pregnancy with you came flooding back. It was strange, the closer we got to the boat and to the tip of the earth, the more flashbacks came and the more I remembered: your conception, my pregnancy, the first days, weeks, and months of your life.

When I found out I was pregnant, I was at home alone, in Edgware. It was a Saturday afternoon. My period was late, and I did a test, just in case. A blue line unexpectedly emerged, as though it was drawn on my horizon, and that day I remembered something Miguel had said: "Without colour life would be a mistake."

BLUE, I wrote in the notebooks:

Blue-blaw, blue blazer and bluebush, navy, turquoise, aquamarine, cerulean, ink-stained fingers. A tiny blue line indicated the pregnancy test was positive. But why does blue equal pregnancy? The Virgin Mary was painted in blue. But blue movies are pornographic. Being blue is feeling sad. Miguel says, "Blue has no dimensions. Blue is beyond dimensions."

Miguel has talked to me so often about colours these conversations are implanted in my mind. They grow like trees; our discussions produce roots and leaves. At La Place, you painted at the kitchen table, saying "My favourite colours are turquoise and purple." I added, "I think blue is the colour of dreams and secrets." Miguel lifted his paintbrush. "When Carl Sagan saw the first photo of the earth from space, he wrote *Pale Blue Dot* to describe our planet. He said we are made of star stuff."

Buba, you interrupted us. You held up your paintbrush. "Mama. Uncle Behind Behind Tomorrow. Blue is the ocean, rain, the sky and it just makes everything brighter. But some blues are sad blues. When we are sad we have these blue stains. They are inside us, but when we cry, the blue goes out."

On the day of my blue line, I got a bus to go and tell Rachel. In her kitchen a cake cooled on a wire rack. She was weighing flour and beating eggs in a bowl.

"It's my colleague's birthday tomorrow. I am making Aunty

Deb's honey cakes." Beside her was a piece of stained paper on which it was written (in Deb's handwriting):

Honey Cake

3 eggs, 1 cup of sugar beat well together

1 tsp cinnamon, ginger, and mixed spice

Add 1lb of hot melted honey, beat well

Stir in 1lb self-raising flour and 1 tsp of bicarbonate of soda

Add 2 cups of boiling water and stir, pour in large tin, put whole almonds on top. Bake 1 hour, 15 minutes. Better eaten on the second day. Improves with age.

"I am pregnant and Antton is the father!" I blurted out, unable to contain my excitement. Rachel screamed and dropped the bowl, and it crashed onto her terracotta floor in a mess of white and honey swirls. "Goodness!" she said. Quietly, I waited for her congratulations, but instead, mop and bucket in hand, she continued,

"Do you want me to get an appointment? I mean, as I have colleagues, I can get you fast-tracked for a termination. It's a simple procedure and I can go with you." She swished the mop back and forth, and I looked at her with shock. The thought of getting an abortion had not crossed my mind. "I am sorry." She noticed my expression, and smiled as though she'd told a bad joke. "It's just… I mean, do you really want a baby now, and have you told Antton? You're twenty-six and finally getting yourself together. I mean does this make sense?"

I put my tea down, grabbed my bag, and walked out, slamming her front door. Without thinking, I turned left and right, the word "sense" shouting inside my head. The area where Rachel and James lived was inhabited by middle-class families: doctors, lawyers, and business owners. I strode past landscaped gardens with flowered things that Rachel called "pergolas" and I teased her she was becoming "far too posh." Rachel's life had followed a trajectory to success. "It is a question of organization," she told me. Prioritising. She had made each moment make sense.

I stopped in front of a house with a Japanese Zen garden; grey and beige pebbles raked into intricate forms. It felt cold and uninviting. How could you "make sense" here, in this area, this world? Sense was a fabrication. Rachel's sense was no better than mine. Her idea that I was "finally getting myself together" was wrong. Most days, I felt like I was biding my time.

I regretted telling Rachel. Of course, I was not against abortion, but I wanted you, *buba*, right from the start, as much as I had wanted anything. I reached the bus shelter, planning to head back to Edgware, and someone grabbed my shoulders. It was Rachel, out of breath. Huffing and puffing, she told me she was sorry, that she loved me, and she just wanted the best. She had never forgotten the day that I had slapped her bully at school, and she would help with the baby, and that our children (her future offspring and mine) could be like cousins, celebrate Passover and Christmas and whatever the Basque people did.

Back at her house, she carried on babbling, made us tea, and cut me a slice of honey cake. She rattled off figures about pregnancy and health, hormones and happiness. When we began to eat the cake, she started to weep,

"I had an abortion last year." Rachel explained she couldn't manage a child before becoming a consultant, but she hadn't told James, because she should have told him before. She went on and on, and I wished she would stop. "I've always admired your freedom," she said, "right from the first day we met. I've never told you, but I've always loved that about you. I am terribly sad about what I said. Really and truly, I apologise."

Years later, Rachel would come and stay with us at La Place, and drive Antton mad chatting nonstop. During her trip James was being interviewed on the BBC about bees, and we listened.

He said:

Bees have multiple roles:

Bees are not born foragers; they only get to do that when they are 14 days old. Before that, they can be:

Cleaners: responsible for brood cells. Undertakers: looking for dead bees to remove them from the hive. Nurses: caring for the queen and larvae. Builders: secreting and producing wax. Temperature Regulators: controlling temperature regulation. Guards: protecting the hive from outside threats.

Rachel was a bee. She had so many roles. *Buba*, when you died, Rachel rang me every day. She came to stay at the house; she cooked and cleaned. For the first time since I had met her, she barely spoke. It was only later, in emails and on the phone that she began to talk about the possibility that I had a form of PTSD. She said this could involve alterations to cognitive processes such as memory, attention, and problem solving. She sent me links to parental bereavements groups and a website where it was written that a violation of one's world of safety could impact a person's ability to resolve grief. She sent an avalanche of information, until Antton told her to stop.

"She's not ready," I heard him tell Rachel on the phone. "She's just not ready."

The day I found out I was pregnant, I finished my tea and gave Rachel a hug. Back home, I told my mum the news, and when I saw her face, I quickly warned her what had happened with Rachel as my mum didn't seem pleased. She just smiled, said "Lovely," and opened a cupboard and her pot of pills.

As for me, nothing prepares you for that moment. When I found out I was pregnant, it was like someone turned on a light. It was a great surprise, as I had never ever longed for children, but, *buba,* time began with you. A new time was starting. The world clock would never be the same. You would be born and have your own clock. You would glow as every living thing radiates.

It was cold and drizzling when we crossed into Brittany. In green valleys, granite cottages crouched on spindly roads. Industrial pork farms rose from muddy enclosures. Artichokes and cauliflowers grew in fields. Neither of us was dressed for the wet and rain. It had been warm when we left the South West, and the temperature dropped by several degrees. The sun came out, and then disappeared. In a cotton summer dress and sandals, I shivered in the car.

"I have some warm clothes on the boat." Yann looked at me with concern. "We should be at the port in three hours. Do you want breakfast?"

I shook my head. The night before, I'd slept badly. Things had sped unhindered in my mind. Each thought connected. A sensation of joy and fear. On my phone, I had another message from Dr. Vidonne. Immediately, I deleted it. Closing my eyes, I thought of you, *buba,* of the Channel and the waves, the roll and the roar. A longing overwhelmed me. For the teal, the verdigris, the is-it-blue or is-it-green? The sea turning a milky copper emerald when a storm is due. My phone beeped. It was a text from my mum. Without reading her message, I turned my phone off. I was advancing toward the boat and the sea and you. Nothing else was of any importance.

"When did you last sail your boat?"

I had been waiting to ask Yann this question for days. He was vague about the last years of his life.

"I think it's four or five years ago. But everything is shipshape. Sylvie promised me she would take care of Little One Hold Tight." I asked again who Sylvie was, but he replied, "She is a pearl and I found her inside an oyster."

Bedraggled and tired, three hours later, we arrived at the port. It was raining. A breeze blew here and there. Waves lapped against a harbour wall. Boats bounced on the swell. Yann parked the car outside a bar.

CHEZ SYLVIE was written in black capital letters above the door. Under a red awning, a group of grey-faced fishermen in yellow waterproof dungarees drank beer and smoked cigarettes. It was eleven in the morning. In the distance, the sea was a muddy green. Rain speckled the windscreen. Yann said,

"We'll set sail tomorrow and leave early to catch the tide." He consulted a tide timetable indicating the times and levels of water. "The tides here are very dangerous and move faster than a galloping horse. The difference between tides is like different worlds." He pointed outside. "Everything can change."

Yann got out, and I went to follow him, but he shook his head. He walked into Chez Sylvie, and the rain fell on the windscreen until the whole world was a blur. Then the sun came out and minutes later Yann ran back out of the bar chased by a young woman. She was in her early twenties, tanned with jet back hair, dressed in a turquoise top, leggings, and heels. Earrings like huge turquoise feathers swung from each side of her head. She carried what looked like a framed painting of a boat. When she eventually caught up with Yann, she crashed the painting over his head and began shouting.

"Why didn't you stay in the hospital and get well? Why haven't you sent news? Five years. I've been so fucking worried. Your bloody boat."

Yann said nothing and stood still as a statue. The boat painting hung like a square collar around his neck. He looked like a condemned man, as though his spine held up his collapsing soul. I thought the woman might push Yann into the sea, but instead she took his hand and pulled him back to the bar, her turquoise earrings jangling. It began to rain again.

In the car, I thought about turquoise. The stone comes from rocks in arid landscapes where groundwater seeps relentlessly, infiltrating volcanic rock. The woman and her earrings were as determined as the colour. Turquoise. Blue.

"Hurry up!" Yann knocked on the car window, gesturing to me to follow him. From the boot, I grabbed my suitcase and notebooks, and walked under the red awning.

"Hello. I am Sylvie. What would you like to drink?" Behind the bar, the woman strode between bottles, cups, and glasses. She seemed wired and wakeful and furious. The place was decorated with sea vessels: pictures of yachts, catamarans, fishing boats, bits of dinghies, and cruise liner souvenirs. On the wall, there was a large gap where I guessed the painting had come from that Sylvie had smashed over Yann's head. Shivering in my cotton dress, I answered quickly.

"A large coffee please." As Sylvie operated the espresso machine, desperate questions flooded my mind:

Why were they fighting?

How did Sylvie and Yann know each other?

Had she looked after the boat?

Could we still cross the Channel in Little One Hold Tight?

Trembling, I sat down, and it felt like everything disintegrated into fragmenting droplets. I felt dizzy. My coffee came slammed down on the table, with a Breton shortbread biscuit. Shivering, I ate it ravenously.

"You look hungry," Sylvie snapped. "Let me make you a sandwich. Ham?" I nodded. She didn't ask me what I was doing with Yann, or why we were here. It felt like she had seen this kind of thing before. Famished, I ate the sandwich and when I had finished, Yann told me, "We're staying here tonight."

He took me through a door by the side of the bar. Stairs led up to a small, bright apartment painted in shades of yellow. He showed me a bedroom with marigold walls. "You look exhausted.

Have a nap, and then we'll go and see the boat."

The yellow walls were a sign, I thought, drifting into sleep, and remembered Frida Kahlo believed yellow was the colour worn by ghosts. Closing my eyes, I walked toward you, Lou. Nobody could stop me; I was travelling toward my golden ghost.

The boat was stored in a lock-up by the port. It was windy and seagulls' cries pierced the air. "She's here," Yann said and with a yank and a rattle, he opened the door, pulled an old tarpaulin off a boat. On the side I read the name: Little One Hold Tight.

"Sylvie looked after the boat. I don't deserve her." Yann had tears in his eyes as he pulled on levers and examined ropes. "She's in perfect condition. I knew that I could trust her. But I think I've let her down." He looked crestfallen, and put his head in his hands. Minutes later, he stood up, turned to me and snapped,

"We'll have to prepare for the journey. We must leave tonight. The lads are bringing the boat to the harbour. You'll need to get organised."

"Yann, everything is great. Thank you." I put my hand on his shoulder.

"You need to get changed." Shrugging me off, he grabbed a bag of old clothes and threw me a pair of men's trousers and a shirt.

When we got back to Sylvie's bar, another group of men knocked back glasses of beer. It had stopped raining. The sky was steel grey and patches of blue broke through the clouds. Upstairs, Yann made me tea and served himself coffee, and I went to ask him a question about Little One Hold Tight, but he held out his hand.

"I need to tell you something, Camille. Sylvie is my daughter. I had a fling with her mother, but I only met Sylvie ten years ago. Beforehand I didn't even know she existed. She came to find me, and when we met I gave her the money for the bar, helped her to make the place look good, paint the walls. We shared this flat for one year. She is a pearl, and I asked her to look after my boat. But—" he put his head in his hands. "We have barely spoken in five years. I let her down, that is why she's angry. I didn't answer her calls because I was ashamed. Things kept going wrong."

"You were ill." I tried to reassure him, but my attempt fell on deaf ears.

"But it's not been enough." Yann drank more coffee; finished the *cafetière*. "She is my home. She was my hope." He looked down into his cup. "I should have been able to do more, shouldn't I? Couldn't I? Camille, I let her down."

In the kitchen, he looked small, like a damaged bird. All the pride fell from him. *Buba,* I wanted to put my arms around him and to tell him as I had told you, everything would be all right. Sylvie would forgive him. I was sure that she would. "You can make things better." But Yann wasn't listening. He kept repeating: "She was my hope." Yann slipped from me and sadness rose from him. If it had been a colour, his sadness would have been blue. A melancholic marine, the blue came from the bottom of the sea; a song of lost love and irreparable mistakes.

Buba, pure blue lacks heat. I wrote this in the notebooks, you knew this, you said: "Mama, colours are everywhere. In your face and your neck. In your hands and feet there are colours. But when you fall over the blue comes up. It comes up and it can come up into your mind and you cry. The blue is very sore."

Objects seen through a blue glass appear to be melancholic. There is something deeply sad about certain blues. In these blues there is an absence of light.

Hearing a noise, I saw Sylvie was listening outside the door. Our eyes met and she put a finger to her lips and beckoned me to join her in the corridor.

"Yann needs rest. I will look after him. He doesn't know what he's saying. But Camille, you'll need to leave us now. You'll have to go back to where you came from." The turquoise earrings swayed.

In her voice, I could hear the message clearly: she wanted me to go, leave the bar, leave the town, leave the region, and leave them alone. But, as far as going back to where I came from, it was impossible. We cannot follow the line of destiny backwards and reverse to reach the start. My home and origins had changed. I couldn't head back to the hospital, to La Place, to Paris, to Edgware, to my mum's house. The only way to move was forwards.

My phone beeped. It was a message from Rachel. I deleted it. As I looked at the yellow walls, I thought of Freud, and something I had read about a moment he describes in the cure, "The lion only leaps once." He was defining an instant to grab, an opportunity, a kind of jump. Beforehand, it is too early. Afterwards, it will be too late. The moment must be seized.

Dr. Rachel didn't believe in psychoanalysis. Said it was "mumbo jumbo. There is no scientific proof." Yann hated "all that talking crap" at the hospital. Yet he never missed a session. Antton believed Freud was one of the greatest thinkers of our time.

As for me, I liked the fact that Freud accepted the messy and welcomed the unpredictable. Since I was a child I had known there were things I couldn't control: my absent father, and my small awkward body. The tears my mum shed when things got too much, and Aunty Deb came over with an envelope of money and barley sugar sweets in a crumpled paper bag. My friends. The Channel. Everything was connected. Everything was something else. Beneath the iceberg, Freud knew that there were things, things at the bottom of the sea, waiting to be discovered. These things could not be calculated. My love for Antton. My pregnancy. Your birth and death.

As I stood in the corridor with Sylvie, this is where I went. My roots were riddles. Memory held ache. Sylvie wanted me to go home, and I knew I could text Antton, book an appointment with Dr. Vidonne. I could return to La Place and finish my grief. I could pop Xanax or Prozac and sleeping tablets every night. In the day, I could teach. "I am back," I could say to the classroom of students and we could voyage among the linguistic tenses, between past, present, and future. I could look at the rose on Monsieur Kassar's desk, but my life would drift into beige.

In the yellow kitchen, the danger I faced was not dying, it was losing my soul. I nodded my head.

"I'll head off tomorrow," I said. Sylvie smiled, and I thought she seemed like a nice person and to want the best for her father. She also didn't seem to know that Yann and I were leaving that night. "Thanks for everything," I told her. *Buba*, I wasn't lying to Sylvie when I said I was leaving, I know I always told you to tell the truth. But I was heading off, and Yann had persuaded me to come this far. "You will follow the crack that is inside you and I will take you wherever you go." We were in this together, and when I walked back into the kitchen, he smiled at me. It felt forced, and he showed too many teeth, giving the appearance of a manic tiger, but he said:

"Camille, I will take you out into the middle of the Channel. Even if it's the last journey I ever make."

Yann's decision made me tremble, and his sadness called to me, his blue incantation of wishes and wants. But, I loved Yann at that moment, and in many more to come. I loved him as I had never loved anyone else. I reached out my hand and stroked his lined face. I hoped that our journey would not push him too far. Yann took my fingers, kissed them gently, and placed them in his palm. Looking deep into each other's eyes, we shook hands.

That evening, as Sylvie worked in the bar downstairs, to the sound of shouts and laughter, we plotted our journey. Tides, currents, latitudes and longitudes, wind, depth, speed, and temperature were calculated. At the sight of my confusion, Yann drew a rough map, saying,

"We'll navigate around the tip of Brittany and stop at Bréhat Island. And then we will cross the Channel." Later, we walked to the late-night supermarket and used our last euros to buy supplies: biscuits, Coke, water, tinned pâté, bread, a dried sausage, sardines, bananas, and a Camembert.

Back at the flat, Yann brought out a waterproof duffle bag, and we filled it with our provisions. I double-checked my notebooks were safely wrapped in the plastic bags. Yann said we would be away for two days and had to go to bed early. "We'll need to get a few hours' sleep. We'll be leaving at midnight."

Yann came into my room. I placed my head on his lap and he gently stroked my hair. When I sat up we kissed each other, and our chaste kiss was unexpected, but when it was over I wanted more.

Before I fell asleep, I kept thinking about Miguel. On my phone, I saw he'd sent texts and tried to call. I knew he was going to Rome, and I thought about a story he'd told me years earlier. He'd sent a letter:

I'm finally in Rome. This morning, I was about to go into the San Francesco a Ripa church to photograph a marble statue I've become obsessed with: the Blessed Ludovica Albertoni. It's an odd piece of art, a Roman noblewoman lying in a sea of sheets. In my guidebook it is written, she "lies on the cusp between two worlds, stilled in the moment of her final breath."

This morning I couldn't enter the building because dozens of women, men, and children were leaving the church, walking down the steps, blocking the way. There was something odd, very quiet about them. Their bodies were almost interlaced. Then, I

saw, in the middle of this silent crowd, four men carrying a very small coffin.

Seemingly from nowhere, people arrived at the square, carrying dozens of bunches of white balloons. They began distributing the balloons until everyone held a silver string with a white balloon attached. A man and a woman walked to the front, I presumed they must be the parents. There was a pause. I almost thought I could hear the whole crowd breathe as one. Then, they let go of their two balloons and they said, "Ciao Paolo!"

After that, everyone followed the same path, their voices joined the parents, "Ciao Paolo!" "Ciao Paolo!" "Ciao Paolo!" "Ciao Paolo!" "Ciao Paolo!" "Ciao Paolo!" "Ciao Paolo!" "Ciao Paolo!" "Ciao Paolo!" "Ciao Paolo!"

The balloons floated into the sky, carried by the voices, the love.

A few hours later, Yann shone a torch in my eyes. Around me the yellow walls glowed. "It's midnight." Gently, he shook my shoulder. "Camille, it is time to go. We must leave to catch the tide." I dressed, ran my fingers through my hair. When I glanced into the bathroom mirror, I noticed my hair was almost back to its normal length. It was strange. I looked like myself again.

In the kitchen, Yann served us coffee, and five minutes later, we crept out into the dense late spring night. Above us, stars lit the sky. We held hands as we walked by the harbour and it felt like we belonged to this night, plans had brought us here, to this place, to find you, *buba*. The night surged from inside me.

Buba, before you were born, everyone warned me about the nights. "You'll be exhausted," Rachel said. "You'll need help," my mum offered. "It might be tiring," Antton frowned. He worried throughout my pregnancy, seeming to think I might collapse.

"It can be relentless," my young and nervous French midwife warned as I approached my due date.

The nights. They say night is a time of moral darkness, of ignorance, for there is an absence of spiritual illumination. When it is dark we see little, but we are also invisible, so we can witness things but our anonymity is retained. Nighttime belongs to floury bakers, to poets, and to white-coated nurses. Night belongs to dancers and twenty-four-hour bars where a woman with smeared mascara asks for just one more drink. The night belongs to lovers, insomniacs, and madmen. Night is an overflow of being, for anything can happen when everyone is sleeping. *Buba,* the night belonged to us.

You were born on the fourteenth of August. My due date had passed, and I had spent the day by the lake with Antton where children kicked sand, adolescent girls adjusted tight bikinis, babies cried, and mothers-in-law tried to make amends. Parasols and picnic boxes. Sun cream and snorkels. Men used water pistols like guns. In the heat we took shelter beneath a tree, and Antton cut a mango and handed me each slice. Sweet yellow, almost-orange. In the afternoon we swam, and my stomach rose from the water like a harvest moon. The lake held me and you, like a secret. You were my unknown.

That evening, after dinner, my waters broke. Antton drove me to the hospital, and I recall the birth: the cries, the body, and limbs turning. Expulsion. Production. Ferocity and softness, turning in circles: the mouth, the pelvis, head, and the vagina.

In the hospital, I wanted to name your birth, and I told Antton, "It is like nothing else." We held you, curled together on a white bed, inside the small box which was our hospital room.

That night, after Antton had gone, I lay watching you, as outside, babies mewed like newborn cats. Lou, you were dappled from the breath of life. You were still part of me. I was still part of you. On the maternity ward, I imagined painting the colours of our conversation in strokes of amaranth purple, Bangladesh green, Bondi blue, mordant red and burnt umber. There was carmine and celadon, cinnabar and cornflower blue, edged with marigold. In the room, the nurses could only see the baby, the plastic crib and the mother. But running round us was a river of life.

Afterwards, the dreaded nights became my favourite time. Antton slept as, dreary-eyed, I lifted you from your crib and slipped out of our bedroom to breastfeed you. Antton bought me a portable radio and, while I breastfed, I listened to the late-night French radio, programmes about the polis: Greek ideals of society and rational thought. Breastfeeding and midnight philosophy complimented each other, like orange and blue. The nights swept around us and we jumped inside.

In the morning, Antton scooped you from my arms. For I hated the daytimes, the bright light, our messy house suddenly visible: the unwashed dishes and dirty clothes. But Antton would get up early and take you around the garden at La Place. As I napped, he whispered the Latin names of flowers in your ears. As dawn broke, the ancient nomenclature enveloped your world. Antton was your day, and I was your night.

We joked about being the moon and the sun. I pumped my milk, and he fed you bottles. I breastfed you once I was awake. Nothing could stop us. Our days were light and flowed carelessly one into the next. But the wheel of fate turned. *Buba*, I know that now. One cannot take things for granted. I should have said *kenahora* at least twenty times a day. A day would come when everything crumbled.

Writing your death feels impossible. Describing that moment seems like a dreadful plan.

In the hospital, Dr. Vidonne told me, "Talking about things can help you heal." Yet I wondered if there were dark places that didn't need light. But, with Dr. Vidonne, I did begin. It was June.

The day before I left the hospital with Yann, she was late for our appointment, and I almost left. But just as I was about to get up and walk away, she came rushing in, and opened her office door. She said, "Anna! Please come in. How are you?"

I started talking...

8. Louis

Dr. Vidonne, I am telling you:

The date is branded in my mind. The twenty-third of September. Antton refuses this date. Despite being a precise person, he says, "I don't want that date in our calendar, as though it were Christmas, or a birthday. I don't want to hold Mass, or light candles. I just wish we could forget."

We argue about this, and I shout, "You don't understand!" Then I'm silent, for the date is engraved in me. My stone is vertical, and it is cold. Every day my fingers trace the chiselled numbers and letters.

I know it is a Sunday because we get up late. Lou and Antton go for a walk by the lake. It is autumn, and the leaves turn orange and red. There is a flood of yellow in the trees. After, there are mushrooms on the kitchen table, a freshly picked basket, naked stems, and a brush of earth. It is a day when it rains, and then the sun shines. A piercing light.

"Perfect mushroom weather," Antton says, and, "I've checked they're not poisonous."

"How?"

"In France you can ask the guy at the local pharmacy."

"Yes, but what if he's wrong?" I am dubious. "Honestly, we should just buy them from the supermarket."

Lou tells me, "Mama, we picked them from beneath pine trees."

The mushrooms are safe, Antton reassures me. They are *cèpes*, chestnut-coloured fungi, precious, and I shouldn't be such a city girl. He irritates me when he calls me "city girl." On that day he says different things, and I will line them up.

Dr. Vidonne, Lou's death marks the middle of my life. There was a before and an after. I carry my *buba* in the middle.

"We can cook the mushrooms with eggs," Antton says.

"Can I break them, Papa?" Lou asks.

Antton nods and Lou fetches an egg from a basket. He taps the egg on a bowl, and his small fingers try to wrench the shell apart. The white and yolk slide down the inside of the glass bowl. The next one, a third, a fourth, and a fifth. The eggs are broken, one by one.

Dr. Vidonne, I am not sure you want to hear this. Why do I need to tell you about the accident? A French philosopher wrote that accidents are surprise. He says as time has accelerated, we no longer understand accidents or the place of death in our lives; we cannot distinguish each colour or emotion. Instead, everything is blurred. On the bookshelves at La Place is Seneca's *Consolations*. He wrote: *it is a surprise accidents don't happen more often.*

Lou beats the eggs. Antton fries the mushrooms and the butter sizzles. The scent of garlic fills the air. The eggs are poured into the pan. Lou is by the kitchen window; he points to the yard at Devant-La-Place. "Look at the chickens," he laughs. "They've gone to the other side."

Dr. Vidonne, he owned his name then. He was called Louis. Lou. After that he was "Lou is dead." There were three words instead of one. Now, his name is stuck to the adjective "dead." An adjective is a word that tells us more about a noun. It describes or modifies. His adjective undid him.

Afterwards, for weeks, when people asked if I had had a better day, or what my plans were for Christmas, or what I thought of the weather or books, or what I did or what had happened to me, all that came to mind was: Lou. Lou is dead. For a long time, I refused to say "dead." People waited, and I said nothing.

There are mushrooms in the morning. Mushrooms dropped in a blackened, cast-iron pan. Butter sizzles with chopped garlic and parsley. Louis stirs with a wooden spoon. He turns it in circles inside the pan.

Grief, I want to shout, Dr. Vidonne, is not a process we go through. Grief drives through us with churning blades. It forces its way through our bodies as though we are the earth and grief is the plough.

Louis cuts the mushrooms with a knife. His father insists that he learns. How to hold a sharp knife and manoeuvre a blade, break eggs and swim in deep water. He was six on that autumn day. He never would be seven. Danger surrounds him.

Dr. Vidonne. In the months after Lou's death, I locked every door in my house, checked for fire, read newspaper headlines, and recorded multiple disasters. It was necessary to try and avoid more accidents, and I looked at online forums for grieving mothers, gathered women dealing with an upside-down world to read the incoherence that no one else will listen to: mushrooms. Sharp knives. Omelettes. An accident.

Lou's absence is pain outside of time. Louis's death is a pain that is time.

It is the twenty-third of September. The sun is shining outside. Fuck the sun, I think in the consulting room with Dr. Vidonne. Fuck that day. Fuck the light, fuck heat, fuck the sky, the clouds, the rain, fuck the brown earth. Nature. Pollution. Fuck sunflowers. Fuck crisps, and breakfast, lunch, and dinner. Fuck the day and night. Fuck time, fuck clocks, fuck mirrors. Fuck the bees, pollinating and connections between all living things. Fuck our house La Place, our middle-class renovation, our aspirations, books, our hopes and dreams. Fuck philosophy. Fuck Orpheus and every single writer who tried to retell a tale of death. Not any death. Fuck those who wrote about what it is like when a child dies. Fuck them. Fuck everyone. Fuck the mothers and fuck the children. Fuck the fathers as well. Fuck the friends and the family with their well-intentioned gestures. Fuck the very ground you walk on. Death is not dignified. Death is not elegant. Death is brutal and death cares for no one. Fuck you all, death says.

In the hallway after lunch, I say, "We'll have a quiet time."

"Yes, Mama," Lou answers.

Were those the last words you said to me? "Yes, Mama." "Yes, Mama." Words translated as thoughts. A word is made of sounds and marks. A word is made of little muscle movements in the throat. His voice, and the last words, "Yes, Mama."

I think those were the last words, and I have replayed the day. I unpick it. Undo the seams, as though the day was a piece of clothing and I take it apart piece by piece, lay out the cloth of the hours and find the pattern, make it again. Avoid accidents. "Yes, Mama."

Two weeks after the accident, I read and re-read the French coroner's report. I look up medical vocabulary on the Internet. In translation, I develop momentary expertise in cranial injuries, bleeding, heartbeats, and causes of death. *Le traumatisme crânien. Lésion. Peau et os.* Skin and bone. The force of the shock, a simple contusion, a bruise or fracture can move the cerebral structures underneath. "Yes, Mama."

It is the quiet time. Siesta time. We all go upstairs, and I go into our bedroom. Antton comes inside. From the hallway, I hear Lou opening his door.

"Papa," he asks, "Can I go and get my ball from the garden?"

"Of course," Antton says. "But then come upstairs quickly, Lou. It's rest time."

I hear his steps on the staircase. The front door opens. Lou goes into sunlight.

Are there units of memory like there are of language? Can I divide the day of his death into smaller and smaller fragments until the core, until the atoms, are held in my hands? Through my remembering, I rekindle the day like fire. The atoms join in a story, and the memory burns.

He goes out into the sunlight. It is a hot day in September. Sudden heat has come, after the rain.

"Perhaps we can go to the lake later?" Antton suggests, and he lies down beside me.

"We could paddle. Lou would love that."

Antton turns and kisses me. We embrace and Antton reaches for me.

Sometimes the only sign that Lou was here is the crack of skin above my pubis. "It is a kiss from you," I tell Lou in the summer, when I am wearing a bikini and he notices the mark, my grey-purple stretch mark. It is a stretching of time, and Lou rose through time, through my time, through me. He rose into me, and out of me. Lou rose. Rose like a flower, and he went outside into the sunlight. It is September the twenty-third. The quiet time.

The day in Paris comes back to me now. Not many parents can identify the precise moment of a child's conception. The skateboarders leap through the air, and in my mind I send them to Hurd's Deep, to the day I met Antton. There was a gap and Lou entered the world as himself. On the twenty-third of September there is another place.

Dr. Vidonne, if the day comes when all my memories of him are stained with this day, with this death, perhaps I will know Lou is really dead. His life will be captured, covered by death. But then he will be alone, and he is only a child. I cannot leave him there. It is impossible to leave a six-year-old alone with their death.

Antton turns to me. Ten minutes have passed. It seems like five or ten. "I am not sure," I later tell the doctor, the nurses, and the policemen. A neighbour. My mother. "I am not sure how long it was before I noticed he hadn't come back." Ten minutes pass. Nothing is sure anymore.

"Did Lou come back in?" I ask Antton. He snores, and I elbow him, then get out of bed, go to Lou's room, and he is not there. I call him, "Lou?" There is a silence. It is too quiet. I call again, "Lou where are you?" It is too quiet.

I am starting from nothing with nothing when everything else has been said…

Without thinking, I go down the staircase, out into the sunlit garden. It is bright outside. The sun is startling. "Lou!" I call again. Now, the silence presses into my pores, and it squeezes against my skin. "Lou!" I shout again, and I run around to the garden at the back of the house. "Lou! Lou!"

I wish we were Hansel and Gretel with pebbles to hedge against the day before and the day after. It would stop us from travelling between these two worlds.

In the garden, by the sunflowers, under the fig tree, is a shoe. I think Lou has left one of his shoes outside. The shoe is in the middle of broken branches by his ball. I look up at the fig tree. I see branches have fallen. On the ground some figs have split; bees gorge on the dripping nectar. Their buzzing sound is all that I hear. I think I will have to pick the shoe up and be careful not to get stung. I reach forward but I see the shoe is attached to Lou's leg. It doesn't seem right. His leg is there with the shoe. His body lies in the grass. Above him is the fig tree and the sunflowers are dry. I notice that straight away and remember soon we will be able to get the seeds from the flower heads. We planned to climb a ladder and shake the sunflowers gently. Lou is lying among the fig branches by his ball. I see he must have climbed the tree, and I think he tried to reach the sunflower heads. I think he must have fallen. His body lies in an awkward angle. His head turns to one side. He has gone but his atoms are everywhere.

I run back into the house and want to scream "Antton." But nothing comes. This has never happened before, and I open my mouth, but I cannot speak, shout, whisper, cannot cry. It is stuck, and I am stuck. Unable to, under water. I am drowning without water. I drown for days, and the words are stuck at the hospital, stuck at the funeral. Nothing is there.

Antton runs into the garden. He makes calls. Antton runs

and makes calls. Kneels. Runs. Stands. Makes calls. There is an ambulance, paramedics, and a doctor. They are touching Louis, beneath the fig tree, among the broken branches by his ball. Antton. Run. Call. I see his lips move, and he is saying something. The doctor speaks. She is wearing a white coat. I don't like this white, and I ask a question to the doctor, "What is your name?" I don't know why I need to know, but it is as though her name is a stone, and I want to throw the stone into this still water, break the surface. I cannot hear her answer.

Months later, when Antton tries to cut the tree down, I am relieved when he fails. The tree must stay standing, by the sunflowers in a row. The figs left in the grass, slowly decomposing.

"Don't touch him," I scream suddenly in the garden with the shoe and Lou lying in the grass. Everyone turns. I try to straighten myself, and I want them to understand I am a good mother. I see Lou's nails are dirty and I wish they were clean, and I want to ask a nurse to bring warm water and soap and a towel. Suddenly, I giggle because I know that if I hold his hand Lou will wake up. He will laugh and tell me it was a joke. No one will know except him and me. The faces around me look shocked when I giggle. I stifle the smile. Somebody comes. They take me from Lou and into the kitchen where they make hot coffee. Add sugar. The doctor enters in her white coat. She talks and gives me an injection in my arm. For shock, they say. It is warm.

In another world, I carry Lou on my back.

Mushrooms. Knives. Omelette. Blue sky. Fig trees. Broken branches. A ball. A fall. A head injury. "Yes, Mama." The quiet time.

At the hospital, I try to look at Antton. We go into the corridor, and we walk. Make calls. A new doctor arrives. "I am so sorry," he says. Do I laugh, or cry, or shake my head? Lou is nowhere and everywhere, and I worry he will get lost in the hospital corridors, I cannot find my way. Doors face more doors, and everything looks the same. I am not sure how to find the exit and to lead him back into the sunshine.

"Yes, Mama."

Dr. Vidonne, in the hospital, I do not think it is the last time that I will see Lou, and I want to touch him, but I don't dare, and I don't know what to do or what to say. I wonder how to speak in French in these circumstances, and then I wonder how to speak in English in these circumstances. I wonder how to speak. Antton says, "He's dead now." He stops and pauses.

We must go home. There has been an accident. Mushrooms. Knives. Omelette. Quiet time. Sunflowers. Broken branches. A fall. Fractured skull. Internal bleeding. The sunlight. It was quick, they said. Quick. Quick.

"Yes, Mama." It was quick.

We go home. Antton cooks. I do not know how he does this. In the kitchen are the mushroom pan and the omelette pan. Antton cooks. I do not know what he cooks or what we eat. Lou's shoes are by the door. His toys. His rabbit. He is everywhere.

It is the evening. I must ring my mum and tell her. Antton stands beside me. I try to find the words, but instead, a wail comes. It rises. A small wail. The wail the size of the death of a six-year-old child.

Dr. Vidonne, the following morning, the day begins, only no one wants its blinding clarity.

[illegible] to look at Anton. We go into the [illegible] and we walk [illegible]. A [illegible] [illegible]

[illegible]

[illegible]

We must go home! [illegible] have not been [illegible] [illegible]

[illegible]

We go [illegible] [illegible] the [illegible] the nurse [illegible] Anton [illegible] do not know what [illegible] or what we eat [illegible] are [illegible] the door [illegible] every [illegible]

In the evening, I [illegible] my [illegible] [illegible] to and the words [illegible] [illegible] small wall [illegible]

Dr. Vidal [illegible] morning the [illegible]

[illegible]

9. Hurd's Deep

Yann had arranged with the fishermen from the bar for the boat to be taken from the lock-up, down the slipway, and into the sea. Little One Hold Tight bobbed in the water. In the moonlight, the boat swayed gently in the breeze. Metal halyards hit masts with a chink.

"The wind isn't as strong as I thought it would be." Yann jumped onto the deck. "We'll have to use the motor. We have a long trip today." He looked from left to right, from his watch up to the sky. "This isn't like your ferry crossings, Camille. It could take us twenty hours to get round the tip of Finistère and out to Bréhat Island. We'll make an overnight stop before heading into the Channel."

Holding my suitcase, I contemplated the gap between the harbour wall and the boat. It felt like a big jump to make in the dark.

"Hurry up. The sky is clear. We need to set sail with the outgoing tide." Yann was insistent, he grabbed my suitcase. Then I leapt, landing in his arms. He clasped me tight, and I felt his fingers on my spine.

"Did you sleep last night?" I whispered in his ear.

"A little." He pulled away, as though he wanted to avoid the question. "The tide is the leader." Muttering about sea levels and pearls, he turned on the motor. "Have to warm her up." He flipped switches and put on the lights, then tossed me a life jacket, a raincoat, and boots. Yann bit his nails. While I got dressed, he unfolded a map, checked his watch and wrote numbers down in a logbook. He undid the knots of the mooring line. I watched in silence as he moved back and forth, pushing and sliding, pulling and attaching.

"We'll raise the sails later," he said. I nodded, impressed.

"Put our bags below," he shouted at me, and threw me a torch. "Now!" he added, and I obeyed his orders. I had spent long enough on ships to know that there is only one captain.

In the cabin, I discovered a small kitchen area, with cupboards, enough beds for four. Everything smelled damp but was clean and organised. When I looked up the moon glowed through the open trap, a globe etched in gold inside a square. I remembered a story Yann had told me during our car journey of "a famous sailor who won an around-the-world race. The guy got there first, crossed the winning line. But when he reached his destination, he decided not to stop. Can you imagine? He went round the world again and again. It's the way to live."

My heart filled with expectation. Perhaps Yann and I could sail and never come back. I put my suitcase with the notebooks on the bed, and an urge overcame me, I removed one and grabbed a pen. By torchlight I wrote:

Dear Buba,

I am finally coming to get you. And I will—

"What are you doing? Get up here!" Yann shouted. "Come and say goodbye to the end of the earth." Leaving my sentence unfinished, I placed the notebook carefully back inside the plastic bags and climbed up the ladder to join him. Everything was dark and quiet, and we sailed into blackness, leaving Audièrne behind. The boat's lights caught the lapping waves. In the distance a lighthouse sent a beam into the night. From here we could see the end of the earth drawn in a twinkle of lights. They got smaller and smaller as we got further away. Everything moved, rocked by the waves. A swing and sway. An inky swell. Silent,

Yann kept his eyes on the water. On the deck, I sat by him, and he took my hand, and we sailed into the great darkness together.

Later, bruised pink edged into the sky, the sun rose, and below the water turned green. Yann ripped open a packet of butter biscuits and handed me four. He ate nothing and swigged from a bottle of Coke.

"I know this area like the back of my hand." Yann pointed at the newly revealed broken-up coastline, scattered with jagged rocks, small coves. "It's a dangerous sail but no harm can come to us." Yann spoke in a low voice, and I shivered as the sky turned bright fuchsia. Orange rays pierced through the end of the night. The dawn was ablaze with scarlet and tangerine. Around us waves suddenly danced, for a brisk wind began to blow. Yann busied himself with the sails. I pulled my hood up and he came, pulled the hood down, and put a black and white striped woolly hat on my head. "Now you're a real Breton sailor."

Soon, we were sailing past what Yann called the Pointe du Raz. In the distance, blade-like rocks rose from a churning sea. "This is the real end of the earth." He began telling me a story about a weekend trip, when he had walked alone round the Pointe. "I almost got blown off the cliff. And the following morning, I couldn't bear the thought of walking back, so I hitched a ride in a fishermen's van. It stank!"

He laughed, but then stopped. The wind was suddenly strong. Yann gripped the wheel, and pointing up, he showed me a final narrow ridge of rock. He shouted so I could hear him above the roar, "They say it's called the Bay of the Departed because of all the people that drowned here. But my grandmother told me it was also because they took the dead druids from here, they sailed them out and buried them on Sein," and he nodded toward an island, out at sea.

We were sailing in a channel between Sein Island and the point. Waves rose, rolled and fell, and rose again. "It's a breeze.

Whitecaps. Spray. Moderate waves. Force 5. Twenty knots. Twenty knots. Force 5," Yann repeated, as though recalling a Yann from another time, as if he had taken a book from a shelf and flipped through its pages only to discover it had already been read. He told me to sit down as he held tight to the ship's wheel, and dials and compasses turned. We entered the open sea.

"The tide is the leader," Yann said. "You must work with the water, with the currents. My grandmother said, 'A sailor carries his life in his hands, and always expects them to be emptied suddenly.'"

I felt my stomach turn and I gripped on to the side of the boat and was sick. "Easy, Camille." Yann looked at me with concern. "It's only a breeze. Perhaps we should have left from another port. We'll be sailing until late." He looked at a chart. "This is the long way round."

"But we had to depart from the end of the earth," I tried to reassure him. Standing on wobbly legs, I put my hand on his shoulder. "There was no other way."

As we sailed into the rough sea, Yann told me the name of the region Finistère comes from the Latin *finis terræ,* meaning the "end of the earth." In Breton, Finistère is called "*Penn Ar Bed,*" which means the "Head of the World." As I began to find my sea legs, I wondered, were we above or below, at an end or a beginning? We were setting out on a journey from a place where everything ended. It was here that everything began.

On our way to Bréhat Island, we crossed paths with fishing boats and dolphins, chatted, ate sardines and bread. The weather calmed and I found the comfort of the sensation when there is no longer sight of any land, just the liquid horizon. In the afternoon, we drank hot coffee from plastic mugs. The sea surface rippled and sparkled. Waves paused and drew out again, and I told Yann, "I've been reading about how when bees leave the hive for the first time, they learn location through a series of flights, navigating their way to pastures and learn the timing of flowers when they release nectar." I sighed, "Can you imagine, each species of flower has a different time?"

Yann said nothing for a while, but he looked at me, and then took his watch off and threw it into the sea. "We should banish all clocks, calendars and look at the insects, the sea. We know nothing about true living." His watch sunk into the water, and I knew he understood. Around Little One Hold Tight, the swell rose, curved, and crashed.

As the sun set, we arrived at Bréhat, mooring the boat in a small harbour tucked on the island's westerly side. "I'm amazed we got this far. You did well." Yann patted the deck of Little One Hold Tight, looked at his boat with pride. We went ashore in a dinghy. In the distance, I made out bright blue shutters, a white façade, and a terrace with parasols. "It's the only hotel on the island," Yann said as we waded onto a beach with pale, almost silky sand. Pine trees grew from behind the dunes, and the scent of mimosa coated the saline air. It was a warm, heady June evening. At the hotel bar, we ordered espresso coffee—the cheapest thing on the menu—and from the terrace we watched the sun set into the balmy sea.

"On holiday?" the waiter asked, and we nodded our heads. When he'd left, Yann reached out and stroked my fingers. "You are very beautiful this evening." His gaze was suddenly blue, and I didn't know what to say or do, for when I looked up his eyes were adamantine. It was a blue that seemed electric, a shocked, crystalline blue, not like the deep sleepy blue of this near to summer day. *Buba*, normally, an adamantine person or thing cannot ever be broken.

The following morning, I was woken early by the smell of fresh coffee. A hand shook my shoulder. "Time to get up, Camille!"

Yann barked. "We must leave the island today, now. There is a storm forecast for tomorrow. We must get going if we want to miss it. Follow the rising tide to get north of the Channel Islands and reach Hurd's Deep." There were lines on his forehead, deep creases round his mouth. Yann looked exhausted, and I told him, "We should stay here and recuperate. It is important we rest before we sail again," and I thought of the maxim "nothing in excess," and I said that if we wanted we could leave the following day. No one was telling us what to do. We were free and could walk the island's sandy lanes, between the white and blue houses; look at the sea over the dunes. We could watch sunsets and drink coffee. We were just beginning…

Buba, I knew you would understand.

But Yann got cross and pointed at the clear sky. "I know what I am talking about. I have my diploma," he snapped. "I am reliable, keep to schedule. The storm is coming." He had black grease on his hands, and I saw he had been working on the motor. A few oily pieces were splayed out on the deck. "Is everything alright?" I asked but he didn't answer and pointed at the sea: "We must leave now. By tomorrow everything will have gone wrong."

When I heard him, I thought of another maxim, "act decisively, do not prevaricate," and I gave in and zipped up my coat. But I should have known better. There is always something wise we can use to justify foolish actions. Yann adjusted switches, wrote numbers in his logbook. Unfolding his map, he drew a path on the chart. "This is where we're going." He pointed north of Guernsey. "Here is the deepest part of the Channel: Hurd's Deep."

With hindsight, I wonder if I should have refused. If I should have listened to his warning that by the next day everything would have failed. Adamantine eyes can be misleading, *buba*. No one is infallible.

At 6:00 a.m. we set sail, left the harbour and white and blue hotel behind. We left the mimosas and the dunes and the sunset walks we would never share. We were heading toward the Channel Islands. "It's where the French Granville fishermen go to fish crabs and lobsters." Yann stared at the open sea. By mid-morning, dark clouds gathered in the sky, illuminated by distant lightning. I got uneasy, for there was something queer and uncanny in the weather, something that I could not account for and didn't understand at all. When Yann turned on the radio, there were coastguard warnings for gale force 5 winds and then gale force 6. Before long, there were warnings for gale forces 7 and 8. Even I knew that it was dangerous. We were sailing into a storm.

I had crossed the Channel dozens of times before but never in a small boat like Little One Hold Tight. The mast shuddered along with the boom. The boat lurched on the waves, tipped at a permanent forty-five-degree angle. Above us, the sky was blown sideways. I was sick constantly. "The lightning is dangerous," Yann shouted. "It will seek out the water. We must stop it setting the boat on fire." He grabbed the anchor chain and wrapped it round the mast, leaving the end trailing in the sea.

"Get inside!" he yelled when I almost fell overboard. I returned to the cabin in the hull. Inside, everything crashed and tumbled. Saucepans had fallen to the floor, knives and forks spilled from an open drawer. My notebooks, inside their plastic wrapper, slid around on the floor. I grabbed the bundle and stuck them into my waterproof trousers.

When I came back out of the cabin, Yann handed me some baguette, ordering me, "Eat." He gulped down Coke while holding tight to the wheel with one hand. One of his eyes twitched. He grimaced as though inflicted by a pain. The waves were rolling, and the boat rolled too,

"We're getting close to Hurd's Deep," he said. It was here that the sea had spoken, carrying a prediction through my days.

Currents and earth's alignments had sent waves crashing onto my shore.

"We're going to capsize," I screamed as the boat veered.

"Hold tight," Yann said. In the darkness we saw a light.

"I can't," I screamed back.

"Little One Hold Tight" he yelled.

I banged my head against the wood as the sail crashed into me. Everything went dark.

Buba, that is when I saw you. You were right before me, in the rain. Your hair was wet. You reached out your hands and called "Mama," and I ran to you, and I held you tight. Our bodies were slippery and wet, and water streamed down your face. I had imagined this moment so many times. I had pictured finding you. Everything was liquid. Water trickled, surged and drifted, ebbed and flowed. It was dark blue, the darkest indigo, for every trace of light had been peeled from here. We were in the shadows, in the water. It was dark and cold, but I held you. Finally. We sank down into the underworld.

Before Orpheus looked back, through the silence of the vast region of shadows, the couple was climbing a wonky staircase, recently renovated by a shady carpenter, who had forgotten his spirit level that day. By the Gates of Tenaro, Orpheus got itchy feet, he lost his cool and was filled with sharp memories of his wife, the photos on his bedside table, a snapshot of her eating a jam doughnut at the seaside, the sweet confiture a sanguine glisten on her lips. He remembered their first kiss outside the Turkish fish and chip shop, with the crispiest batter in northwest London. He thought of their wedding day.

When Orpheus looked back, he turned from the present and the future, and moved his gaze nostalgically to what had once been. He clung to an illusion.

When Orpheus looked back, Eurydice died a second time,

and she raised her eyebrows, as though, some claim, she had known what was coming. She knew Orpheus well, he had a sentimental side. Yet, she was generous, and before she returned to the underworld, she reached into her pocket, and she showed him a screenshot on her phone, a picture she had taken of trees.

He wept. "It's all over."

But Eurydice sighed, "You're mistaken. Everything is alive." Before descending to Hades, she handed him an indestructible light bulb, and between them the light shone like an infinite star.

As we sank, you whispered, "Mama, you have to stop looking back."

"But *buba*, you're in my past." I was breathless, trying to explain that if I stopped looking back, you would disappear. If I accepted your death, you would be forgotten. If I held tight to the past, nothing changed. The dust could grow thick on every tree, book, and thought. But you would be remembered.

Buba, you pulled me, yanked at my arms. I felt a tearing inside me, between the part of me stuck in what had been and the part of me being pulled into the future. "We have to let go," you said. But the effort was too great. It was asking too much, asking a grieving mother to walk into the future with her dead son.

"He is here," shouted voices, and three figures swam toward us: Antton's mother Katixa, Aunty Deb, and Princess Diana. Aunty Deb wore scarlet and purple, Princess Diana was in her clementine suit, and Katixa had thrown off her black mourning cape and had put on a blue dress. They swam round me like fish. While I clung to you, they muttered about living with the dead, situating history in the present, death being a part of life. The trio spun, and the thread from their clothes wound into my limbs, pulling and stitching everything together.

Then I noticed a bee turning in the water, then a second, a third. A swarm of bees were with the women swimming in a circle, and as they spun, the wheel of colour turned. While I stared at the chromatic rush, Aunty Deb grabbed the orange notebooks from me. Flipping through my drawings and notes, she began shredding the pages about beige, the theories about the trench coat. More and more bees arrived until the blue water was thick with insects, moving together, around us, and I reached out and tried to take the notebooks back from Aunty Deb, but Katixa joined in, and then Lady Diana. They ripped out the obituaries and all my ramblings.

"Stop!" I shouted, though what came from my mouth was a gurgle as we sank deeper into the sea and the waves of bees. It was a relief to sink. I sank deeper than I had ever gone before.

Suddenly, I was next to you. *Buba*, we walked together, advancing in time, carried on the stream of bees. I clasped your small fingers. You looked up at me, and I looked at you, and you were with me. No one would ever take you away. It was our secret. Something I now accepted I could tell no one. The only place it could exist was in these orange notebooks. I could live with your death, *buba*, in the knowledge that you were here beside me, held by the bees. Like Orpheus I shouldn't look back, shouldn't stick you in the past, in the scrapbook of time. When I was pregnant I had carried your time within me. When you were born, my time had changed. When you died, everything had stopped. This was grief. Grief was time. Now, you could be a carried-again child. Time would flow again. The bees and the women would link us together. Connect. Pollinate.

Katixa said, "Open your eyes. The bees are here."

Yet I couldn't. It was much easier to keep them closed and to stay with you, *buba*, as we stepped along the underwater valley of Hurd's Deep. The clocks turned. Rivers flowed. Flowers opened and closed. Bees timed the releasing of nectar. People were born and died. It was impossible to know what would happen next. Would boats capsize, would lives be lost? Would the gods bless the day? Would you stay with me? The bees covered us, the swarm grew thicker and thicker, until I couldn't see anything. I clasped your hands, and words came, those that had been locked between my lips, babble and chatter poured out of me. Then, Aunty Deb, Katixa, and Lady Diana shouted together,

"Open your eyes."

Reluctantly, I did what they said.

I found myself lying flat on my back on the slippery deck of a fishing boat, surrounded by plastic crates crammed full of lobsters and crabs. "Open your eyes," a sailor was shouting, and Yann was beside me. I heard voices bellowing "Nice haul!" Pincers opened and closed. I didn't know if what had happened was real or a dream. Where were the three women? The bees? Where was Lou?

"Where is Little One Hold Tight?" Yann shouted, thrashing from side to side, "Where is Little One Hold Tight?" He stood up, skidded, and fell back onto the deck.

"We're towing your boat," one of the fishermen said, gruffly. "You're lucky to be alive." By the time the fishermen got us back to Granville port, Yann was screaming about wanting to return to the middle of the Channel with Little One Hold Tight. "I must keep on sailing around the world. Again and again." Lurching, he tried to jump over the side of the boat; the fisherman held him down.

At Granville port, they called for an ambulance. By the cliffs of the old town, next to the rows of seafood restaurants, I watched in horror as he was given a sedative. Following a consultation with a psychiatrist, as I would find out later, Yann was sectioned, considered as a danger to himself. "Camille!" he yelled as they took him into the ambulance, "Don't let them lock me up again. Don't let them lock me up. The stars are calling. I am a skipper. I need to sail. I must be on the water, sail around the world with you. Please help me. Camille! Help me!"

Yann pulled at his hair and beat the air around him. Waving his arms, he wept. A white trail of saliva ran from one side of his mouth. Passing groups of tourists stared, and I wanted to tell them to look away. Yann had lost control, and I had never seen him like this before, or perhaps for the first time I saw his illness, as though something lifted from my eyes, as though for weeks and months I had been blind to myself and Yann's difficulties. Suddenly, I realised I needed to tell him about my dream, about what had happened in the middle of the sea. But the ambulance door closed behind him, and it began to drive away.

"Please could you stop the ambulance?" I asked one of the fishermen, "Please, it's important. I need to talk to my friend. I shouldn't leave him alone. He's not well and he's a good man. A very good man." The fisherman shook his head.

Another ambulance arrived and they took me to the general hospital, but apart from a few scrapes and bruises everything was fine. The nurses told me I could be discharged. When I left the hospital, I was trembling, but said, "I am fine. All is good."

I didn't know where to go or what to do. The hospital was outside of town. The fisherman had salvaged my suitcase from the boat. I had my notebooks, my purse, and my phone. On the main road, I caught the first bus that arrived. In Granville, I walked around the streets, through the centre, up to the ramparts and the old town. In the cobbled streets, I remembered that I could use my credit cards and saw that no one was following me, or ever had. There hadn't been hidden microphones or the CIA. It was confusing. Why had I believed everything Yann had said?

It began to rain heavily, water falling in thick drops from the sky. Men and women opened umbrellas, put up hoods, and closed coats. But I walked on with my suitcase getting wetter and wetter as though nothing could touch me, as though nothing ever would. Then, I found myself inside a small supermarket.

After walking around the aisles, I bought a bottle of whisky. At a cash machine, I withdrew money, and in another shop I bought jeans, underwear, a T-shirt, and a pair of bright red pyjamas. I put everything inside my suitcase, did each action like I was a walking ghost. *Buba*, so many things were dawning on me, but I wasn't ready to face it all.

Without warning, the sun came out. A blue sky chased the clouds away, and in the streets I turned away from the sea. Down a hill, I found myself by the railway station, and I stopped in front of a hotel, The Quay's End. It was next to a Turkish take-away. The air smelt of cooking fat. Seagulls pulled greasy balls of paper from a bin.

Bright sunlight glared on the sodden streets. Tarmac shimmered from the recent rain. Dizzy, I leant against the hotel wall. My head stopped spinning, and I almost turned and walked away, thought I would jump on the first train leaving the station, try and find an airport and catch a plane. I was by the edge of the Channel, and I needed to leave. I thought I could flee, go anywhere. The doctor at the hospital had warned me, "You've had a shock. You must make sure you rest." I pushed open the hotel door.

"I am on holiday; I'll just be staying one or two nights," I explained to the trio behind the reception, a skinny white French man, a small Vietnamese woman, and a large, overweight Labrador. It growled.

"Be quiet, Van," the woman told the dog, and glanced at me. "He's named after Van Gogh." Behind the reception were framed pictures of the Normandy coast and Granville, seascapes painted in garish shades of yellow and lime green. The walls of the hotel were lilac.

"My wife is a painter," the man said. I nodded. The woman explained the only available room was on the fourth floor, with a view of the inner courtyard. The dog growled again, and then the man shouted, "Quiet, Van!" The woman smiled at me. "Good luck."

Inside the lift, I placed my fingers on the number four, and as it rose, I kept wondering why the woman had wished me good luck. Did she know where I had been? Inside my room, my first thought was that I had to get clean, wash the journey from me. But first, I opened the whisky and took a gulp. It burnt, but I took a second mouthful. In the tiny bathroom, I turned the shower on, and I washed myself again and again. As I scrubbed the flashbacks of your funeral returned and something I had written in the notebooks. This time I let the memories come. I no longer fought against them. You were my wound, *buba*, I needed to dress you and let you heal.

I had written:

They had told us it would take one hour to burn your body. We had chosen a cremation, somehow I thought it would make things lighter, make you lighter. They said we could have a funeral and bury your ashes. I thought after your cremation I would be air bound. Instead, afterwards, all I felt was weight. The weight of your fall. We fall in love, fall pregnant, and fall sick and die. You fell.

Everything, I thought, as I turned off the shower, is bound by gravity.

I put on the clean pyjamas. The red fabric felt soft and new. But, when I lifted my hand I saw I was trembling. I crept into bed and drank more whisky, and decided to contact the psychiatric hospital, but the nurse on the phone told me Yann was in a closed ward and not fit for visitors. I rang Sylvie at the bar, and she shouted down the phone, saying Little One Hold Tight was irreparable. She told me I had led Yann astray and that I should never try and see him again.

Under the covers, all that I could think about was Yann. Somewhere in another place, in a closed ward, he must have struggled and fought. Nurses would have sedated him with a forced injection, and he would be drifting into a chemical sleep. I regretted agreeing to travel with him to the middle of the Channel. It was selfish and destructive, for Yann had fallen apart.

Throughout the night, as soon as I closed my eyes, I pictured myself holding his hands, and I calmed the nervous terror shooting through his veins.

"I am here," I promised Yann, repeatedly, as the moon lit the sky and stars sprinkled yellow into the night. "Yann, I have not forgotten you." In the darkness, I put my lips to his and held him tight.

When I woke in the Granville hotel the following morning, it was to the sound of seagulls. I was crying and crying, and I could not stop. In the bed, I cried for Yann and for all that had gone wrong. I cried for Lou, for Hurd's Deep, for had we really met? I cried for Antton and my stupid recklessness. I cried for Lady Diana and Aunty Deb. In the hours that followed, everything collapsed, or was released. I didn't really know which it was.

"You can cry," I remembered Dr. Vidonne had told me. "Tears are the unsaid words."

It was 4:00 a.m., too early for breakfast, I couldn't get back to sleep. I opened the orange notebooks. On my hotel bed, I turned the damp pages. Much of the writing was smudged and barely decipherable: snatches of paragraphs, "beige is evil," recipes, memories of Lou, Lala, the chickens, obituaries. I began wondering what had happened. Nothing in these pages made any sense. Frustrated, I tossed the notebooks to the floor. Picking up my phone, I noticed new texts had arrived from Miguel that I hadn't deleted. I read them, one after the next...

My Anna, Where are you? Antton is so worried. He says you left the hospital. You must send news darling. He loves you. We all love you. Call.

Then another:

You keep asking about colour in your emails? Do I answer as your old friend (I AM VERY WORRIED) or as a painter? My new paintings are monochrome. It is the line that interests me. My lines are never broken. I refuse breakage. My boyfriend says this is Tao: life does not end.

Another:

Anna, please CALL, but I'll text about other things: you ask: "What do you think of beige?" Recently, I read 2 researchers found the colour of the universe. They took light samples of all the different colours emitted from galaxies. Their research shows that the main colour of the universe is beige.

On the hotel bed, I put my hands over my mouth. I wanted to throw the phone down but I couldn't. I had to continue reading the final (longer) text from Miguel:

Anna, I so often think of Lou. I painted the sunflowers with him.

"They are light," he said. I never forget. I have sunflowers here. I planted them for Lou. At night, they turn east. Flowers do this until they get old, when they stop moving. Then, old flowers wait for bees that will spread their pollen and make new sunflowers. Those flowers too will follow the sun.

Anna, we can follow the sun and stand in the daylight as well as the night. Without light there is no colour, without day there is no night.

Anna, you must know colour is light.
Listen to the flowers. CALL ANTTON!
Love U
Miguel

There are some things to which there are no responses, even to oneself. When I finished reading, I went and looked out of the hotel window. The sun rose in the east. The day was beginning. Suddenly, I wished I could see Miguel. I wished he were here, with Rachel and my mum. But most of all I wanted to see Antton, I wanted to tell him: *the day is beginning.*

Crossing the road to the railway station, I booked a train ticket back to La Place. It seemed like it was time to go home. I texted Antton. *I am fine, I am so sorry.* I didn't tell him about the journey, about nearly drowning, about Lou, about the three women in the sea or the bees. When I thought of it now, the women reminded me of the threnody, the Etruscan female link between life and death. Flipping through the pages of the notebook, I stared at the orange and red Etruscan mural, the postcard Miguel had sent me from Rome. The line of ancient grieving women advanced together through time. They held onto each other as they grieved, and that was all we really could do, and the continuity made all the difference. We needed to keep death in life. We couldn't banish it underground. But we had to connect with each other, make our own new stories, mix the living and the dead. Invent our rituals. Embrace it all. Bees and boys. Three thousand years later, we were still dying, and *buba,* I still felt your hand in mine.

10. The Light Did Find at Last the Mirror of a Woman

"Life is that group of functions which resist death."

Marie-Francoise Xavier, *Physiological Research upon Life and Death,* 1800

We have arrived at the end of this orange notebook. There are only a couple of empty pages left. I don't want to stop writing but things have a beginning, middle and end. There is only enough space left for another few hundred words. I think of something Dr. Vidonne said: "We are all born again and again, our selves evolving like the clouds or the sea." I glance into Lou's mirror. It has caught the light, and is illuminating shadows, the souls of the strung-up, and the glisten of a slowly ending day. My face seems different somehow.

Antton will be home soon, and for now, I need to shower and unpack my bag. There is one thing I haven't written about yet.

Before I left to go on the journey with Yann, I came home to La Place and Antton made the Basque fish stew and we spent the night together as we hadn't done for months. Weeks have passed. My period is late.

At first, I thought it was due to medication and shock. But before I caught my train, I went to a pharmacy and bought a pregnancy test. In my hotel room, I urinated on a white plastic stick. After five minutes, a blue line appeared in the white circle.

Blue used to be the most expensive pigment, the most difficult to make. Blue is the azure for which the Greeks had no word, no terminology for this colour of life.

As I write this I keep looking out of the window in Lou's bedroom. The sun is setting. Deep pink streaks cross the sky. Every minute things change, appearing and disappearing. Things are being born and going away. If I stand by the window, I will see Devant-La-Place, the chickens, and the land that hides the lake. It is June and the trees are fully leafed. The sunflowers reach into the sky, and soon it will be night and we'll sleep.

At dawn, our eyes will open and harvest light. The eye perceives millions of colours in one flash. They say our sense of light evolved from touch, to anticipate danger and recognize reward. But the human eye also gathers beauty, marvels at a garden bathed in copper light.

In Lou's bedroom, I wait for Antton to walk up the path. He will stride between the lavender bushes and bees. The bees will surround him, flying in patterns made from flower time, a clock of releasing nectar. Antton will open the front door and walk up the stairs. The books will line the steps and a new page will be ready. Our imperfect, rough invention. Lou will be with us, and we will walk hand in hand, and not look back. I will take Antton in my arms, and I will tell him:

It is a different time. It is the carried-again child time. The dead time. The time that is life. The Etruscan threnody have been singing mystery for three thousand years. Baking biscuits for the living and the dead. I hope Antton will understand.

When I am done I have to decide what do with these orange notebooks. Keep them? Throw them away? Or put each and every one inside an envelope and post the notebooks to Dr. Vidonne? I wonder if she could be the guardian, keep watch at the gate. For we all need to be heard, held, seen, and read. Our words must belong in a library somewhere.

I wonder whether I will be inconsolable forever. Perhaps my pain is my way to hold onto this love. Soon, in the garden, four sunflowers will tilt toward the sky. We can go on. I think we can...

Acknowledgements

Grateful acknowledgments are made for their generous help to Dr. Dave Goulson (on bees) and to Basque anthropologists Dr. Isabelle Mellén and Dr. Susana Carro-Ripalda. *Un grand merci* to J.P and Dr. C for sharing your invaluable clinical experience.

Many thanks to early readers: Seraphina Madsen, Sam Mills, and David Collard for your sharp eyes, hearts and rigorous minds. Part of *The Orange Notebooks* was written during a fellowship at the Hawthornden Castle, and I would like to thank the incredible staff and my fellow writers.

It's been a great privilege to work on *The Orange Notebooks* with my wonderful editor, Leonora Rustamova, excellent publisher Kevin Duffy, and the Bluemoose team, and for the North American edition of *The Orange Notebooks* with the wonderful Assembly Press team. Many thanks to them for taking care of this book.

As ever, I thank my brilliant agent Jessica Craig for her belief in this book and my writing.

All gratitude to A and our three daughters.

Last, but not least, none of this would be possible without the living *and* the dead. This book is for both.

Photo credit: Morgane Michotte

Susanna Crossman is an essayist and award-winning fiction writer. Her acclaimed memoir, *Home is Where We Start: Growing Up In The Fallout of The Utopian Dream,* was published by Fig Tree, Penguin, in 2024. She has recent work in *Aeon, The Guardian, Paris Review, Vogue,* and more. A published novelist in France, she regularly collaborates with artists. When she's not writing, she works on three continents as a lecturer and clinical arts-therapist. Born in the UK, Susanna Crossman grew up in an international commune and now lives in France with her partner and three daughters.

Printed by Imprimerie Gauvin
Gatineau, Québec